Trap

The gigantic mantis swung its claw, and Hunter ducked. The claw flashed over his head, biting into the tree. Hunter staggered around the tree trunk, trying to put it between himself and the mantis.

The bug hissed and shrieked, trying to catch Hunter. Hunter started to bolt deeper into the jungle, but a huge spider emerged from the foliage.

It was a sleek, colorful arachnid, nearly the size of an elephant. Hunter froze in his tracks, staring in amazement.

Standing on the back of the spider, riding it as though it were a huge surfboard, was a girl. A large silver bracelet covered with spider designs encircled her right wrist.

Hunter stood trapped with his back to the tree, caught between the mantis and the spider. Was the girl controlling these hideous insectoids? Was she the ruler of this place?

The girl's liquid eyes burned with hatred and cold determination.

Hunter knew that he was doomed.

The girl surged forward on her horrible beast, her eyes narrowed. She drew her spear and hoisted it to shoulder height. "Venus, attack!" she cried.

SPIDER RIDERS
The Shards of the Oracle

by Tedd Anasti and
Patsy Cameron-Anasti

with Stephen D. Sullivan

A Cookie Jar Entertainment Book
Newmarket Press • New York

> **Acknowledgments**
> Grateful acknowledgment is made to the following for their assistance in the preparation of this book: Tedd Anasti and Patsy Cameron-Anasti for creating the world of the Spider Riders; project editor Anne Greenberg for overseeing all of the details; Stephen D. Sullivan for his writing expertise; and, especially, Toper Taylor, whose inspiration and leadership made this book possible, along with his dedicated staff contributors at Cookie Jar Entertainment: Travis Williams, Mike Wrenn, Kelly Elwood, and Fonda Snyder.

Copyright © 2004 by Cookie Jar Entertainment Inc. All rights reserved.
Spider Riders™ Cookie Jar Entertainment Inc.

All rights reserved. This book may not be reproduced, in whole or in part, in any form, without written permission. Inquiries should be addressed to Permissions Department, Newmarket Press, 18 East 48th Street, New York, NY 10017.

This book is published in the United States of America.

First Edition

ISBN 1-55704-652-2 (paperback)

10 9 8 7 6 5 4 3 2 1

ISBN 1-55704-653-0 (hardcover)

10 9 8 7 6 5 4 3 2 1

Library of Congress Cataloging-in-Publication Data available upon request.

QUANTITY PURCHASES
Companies, professional groups, clubs, and other organizations may qualify for special terms when ordering quantities of this title. For information, write Special Sales Department, Newmarket Press, 18 East 48th Street, New York, NY 10017; call (212) 832-3575; fax (212) 832-3629; or e-mail mailbox@newmarketpress.com.

www.newmarketpress.com

Manufactured in the United States of America.

*For Emily Rose and Teddy,
our young children,
whose love of spiders inspired this novel*

CONTENTS

PART ONE: THE INNER WORLD

1. Hunter Steele 3
2. The Long Slide 8
3. Spider Rider 16
4. Captive! 22
5. Land of the Spiders 28
6. Riders to the Rescue 36
7. Into the Fire 42
8. Trapped Between Fire and Water 52
9. A Wave of Victory 59
10. The Breakout 70
11. The Spy 76

PART TWO: SPIDER RIDERS

12. Spider Canyon 85
13. Hunting Spiders 91
14. Specters of Doom 100
15. Shadow 108
16. Nest of the Roach 116
17. The Second Shard 122
18. Shadow and Darkness 131

PART THREE: THE BATTLE FOR ARACHNIA

19. A New Rider......................... 145
20. The Lost Legion 156
21. The Snowmites' Trap.................. 167
22. The Third Shard 173
23. Shadow from Above 180
24. City Under Siege..................... 189
25. Lightning Attack..................... 197
26. Hunter Fights Alone 203
27. A Hero's Welcome................... 209

PART ONE

THE INNER WORLD

1
Hunter Steele

"I am *not* afraid of spiders!" Hunter Steele told himself as he hiked across the rugged hillside. The forested countryside behind his home stretched out ahead of him, reaching into the mountains beyond. The woods were old and tangled and filled with unpleasant wild creatures—like spiders. Hunter tried hard not to think about that as he trudged forward.

"Come on, Hunter! Keep up!" Dave called. Hunter's friend hiked up the rocky slope, heading for the ridgeline. "We've never been up this way before," he said. "If we're lucky, maybe we'll find an old mine or hidden treasure or something."

"Yeah," Hunter said. "If we're lucky." He smiled halfheartedly. Discovering lost treasure would be nice, but Hunter had no desire to find any mines. Mines were dark and cramped and filled with all kinds of creepy things—like spiders. Hunter mentally ran through a catalog of what kind of spiders might live in an old mine.

Because he didn't like spiders, Hunter had made it his business to know about them. "Know your enemy," his dad had once said—not about spiders, about something completely different. But the same idea applied to spiders. So Hunter knew all about them: spider types, spider lairs, spider body parts...all that creepy kind of stuff. Knowing about the eight-legged fiends didn't make him like spiders any better, though.

Hunter scrambled up the rocky slope behind Dave, trying not to appear chicken. Dave liked to tease Hunter about his fear of spiders. If Dave guessed that Hunter was worrying about spiders now, Hunter would never hear the end of it.

"Hey, would you look at that!" Dave said. He was standing at the top of the ridge, his hands propped on his hips.

"Look at what?" Hunter asked, still a few yards behind his friend. He hoped that Dave wasn't seeing an old mine filled with black widows, orb weavers, trapdoor spiders, brown recluses, and all other manner of horrible arachnids. "What is it?" he repeated.

Dave shrugged. "I don't know," he said. "It might be an old gravel pit or something."

Hunter reached the top of the slope and gazed down into the pit. It looked like a huge bowl—fifteen yards across—filled with loose rock and sand. The depression took up the entire top of the ridge, blocking the way into the mountains beyond. The pine trees stopped at the rim of the pit, ringing the hole like lonely sentinels.

"Maybe it's an old volcano cone," Hunter suggested. "There are some extinct volcanoes in these parts."

"Or maybe it's what's left of an old pit mine," Dave said. "They used to dig mines like that. I heard they dug one so deep that it hit an underground spring. The pit filled up with water and became a lake."

Hunter laughed. "I guess they didn't dig this one deep enough," he said. "Too bad, or we could have gone swimming." The summer day felt warm enough for a swim, and both boys were sweating from their long climb.

"Yeah, too bad," Dave agreed. "A dip would have felt nice."

Hunter walked around the edge of the pit, balancing on the big rocks at the rim.

"Hey," Dave said, "that might be dangerous. If you fell in. . ."

"If I fell in," Hunter interjected, "I'd roll to the bottom and get scraped up. Big deal. These are old clothes, anyway."

Dave smiled and started walking around the rim of the crater behind Hunter. "If this was a mine," he said, "I wonder what they were mining."

"Rocks, it looks like," Hunter said wryly.

"Tiny gray, boring rocks," Dave added. "I hear they pay a lot of money for those." Both boys laughed.

"Maybe we should grab some," Hunter said. "We could be tiny gray rock zillionaires!"

Dave crouched down on the rim, reached into the pit, and scooped up a handful of the loose pebbles. "Look at me," he said. "I'm striking it rich!" He threw the tiny stones up into the air and yelled, "I'm a zillionaire!"

As he did, he lost his balance on the edge of the rim.

"Whoa!" Dave yelped as he toppled into the wide gravel bowl. Before Hunter could grab him, Dave rolled down the slope, toward the center of the crater.

"Dave!" Hunter cried. He hopped off the rocky ledge and scrambled down the side after his friend.

The tiny, loose rocks slid out from under Hunter's sneakers. Only his keen sense of balance kept him from tumbling head over heels after his friend.

"Hunter!" Dave called. He reached out his hands as he slid toward the center of the deep gravel bowl.

Hunter's eyes went wide. The gravel was sliding too, now.

It was vanishing down the center of the bowl, like water running down a drain.

"Hang on, Dave," Hunter cried. Fighting to stay on his feet, he leaped down the slope after his friend.

Dave eyed the hole opening up near the bottom of the pit. "Hurry!" he shouted.

Hunter threw himself forward onto the sand and gravel. He landed hard on his stomach, reached out, and grabbed Dave's hands. Both boys skidded to a stop. Dave looked over his shoulder into the center of the pit. The gravel and sand kept moving, trying to pull him under.

"Crawl as hard as you can!" Hunter said. He pulled Dave's arms, and his friend scrambled up the slope toward him.

"Keep going," Hunter urged. He helped Dave climb past him and pushed his friend toward the top of the slope. Dave's hands grabbed the rim of the pit. Hunter crawled up after him.

Dave pulled himself up onto one of the big, flat stones at the crater's edge. He lay there, panting for a moment, then turned back and reached out for Hunter.

Dave didn't notice the delicate spiderweb clinging to the weeds at the pit's edge. He didn't notice as he pushed his hand right through the web, disturbing its occupant. Dave stretched his hand downward, giving Hunter something to grab onto.

"I've got you!" Dave said. "Grab hold!"

Hunter reached out and seized Dave's fingers. The gravel gave way beneath Hunter as the rubble and sand slid down into the ever-widening hole at the center of the pit.

He nearly skidded back, but Dave held tight. Hunter glanced back at the pit he'd narrowly escaped. He let out a long sigh of relief. Then he spotted the spider.

Hunter Steele's heart went cold. Dave didn't see the fingernail-size yellow-and-black spider crawling down his arm toward Hunter.

Sweat broke out on Hunter's forehead. "A common garden spider," he told himself. "Not dangerous at all...not venomous...not..."

The spider crawled off Dave's arm and onto Hunter's hand.

"Argh!" Hunter cried. His fingers flew open reflexively as he tried to shake the spider off.

"Hunter, no!" Dave cried as their hands slipped apart.

Hunter tried to grab Dave again, but it was too late. Hunter slid down the gravel like a sled on an ice-covered mountain.

He twisted around, trying to regain his feet.

The bottom of the crater yawned before him, a hungry mouth beckoning. The gravel slid into it, like sand through an hourglass.

Before he could stop himself, Hunter plunged through the hole.

Dave's frightened scream followed him down.

"Hunter...!"

2
The Long Slide

Sand and gravel covered Hunter's head, and darkness closed in around him.

For a few moments, he heard Dave shouting his name. Then the rush of the falling sand and gravel filled his ears.

Hunter felt as though he were drowning in dirt. He wondered for a moment if anyone would be able to dig him out before he suffocated. Dust and grit caked his eyes and choked his lungs.

Then, suddenly, he was falling through empty air into a dark space below the earth.

He screamed.

The scream echoed around him as he plunged into an icy river.

Hunter coughed and sputtered. He kicked his feet and broke the surface of a raging, underground watercourse. It was still pitch-black. He couldn't see anything.

He tried to swim for the shore, but he couldn't tell which direction to go. It was like being on a water park ride at night, wearing a blindfold. During daylight the experience might have been fun, but instead it felt incredibly scary.

Hunter kept swimming, barely keeping his head above water, hoping he wouldn't crash into anything. He heard the sound of water rushing around rocks but couldn't see them.

At any moment, he expected to slam into something with bone-crunching force.

He fought down the fear. "Just keep going," he told himself. "This has to end sometime."

A roaring sound echoed ahead of him, and a red glow gradually appeared in the distance. Hunter realized that he was in a long, tubelike tunnel at least five yards wide. The wide stream he'd been caught in rushed down the middle of it. The tunnel's stone walls sloped up steeply. He saw no way to crawl out of the water.

The red-orange glow at the far end of the tunnel grew brighter as the river carried him forward.

"It looks like fire," Hunter thought. A scary idea shot through his brain. "It might be *lava!*"

Hunter had seen old volcanoes near his home. What if he'd stumbled into one? What if he was rushing straight toward the burning heart of the mountain?

He tried to grab hold of the tunnel wall to slow himself down, but the stone had been worn smooth by water and time. He bruised his fingers against the rocks but didn't slow down one bit.

Hunter thought about the waterslides he'd been to on family vacations. He remembered that if you spread your legs and sat up, you would slow down. He fought the force of the water and managed to pull himself upright.

He slowed somewhat and also got a better look ahead. In the distance, the tunnel widened into some kind of huge vertical shaft. Hunter didn't like the look of that opening. The rocks of the cavern shone with gleaming red light, reflected up from below.

"Definitely lava," Hunter thought. He glanced from side to side, determined to find a way out, trying not to panic. The huge fiery shaft loomed closer by the second. Hunter's heart pounded in his chest. He tried not to think of falling into the lava pit ahead.

His frantic eyes lit upon a dark blotch on one wall near the end of the tunnel. Just before the opening, a smaller passage branched off to the right.

As the end of the main tunnel rushed toward him, Hunter stuck out his hands, dragging them on the wall, trying to control his slide. The tunnel opened up, growing higher as it entered the towering shaft beyond. Hunter twisted his body, angling toward the side passage. He was going too fast! He was going to slip past it!

He stabbed out with his hands, trying to grab the wall. His fingers skidded over the lip of the side passage entrance.

For a moment, Hunter pictured himself flying through the air and falling into the lava shaft ahead, but the friction of his hands turned him just enough. He left the main passageway just before it entered the towering vertical shaft.

Hunter barreled into the smaller chute, hardly able to believe he'd escaped certain doom. Behind him, water gushed out of the main tunnel and into the empty air, becoming a spectacular waterfall tumbling into the molten lava at the bottom of the shaft.

The hiss of the water turning into steam filled Hunter's ears as he shot into the side passage. He caught his breath as the air around him cooled once more. It began getting dark again, too. This time, though, tiny points of light glittered in the blackness.

"Minerals in the rock," Hunter told himself. He felt comforted by the starlike lights. Wherever he might be headed, he wouldn't be completely in the dark.

"I'm going to make it through this," he said to himself. "I won't give up. I'm going to reach the end of this slide and get back home."

This new tube through the rock was as smooth as the first, though much smaller—barely wider than Hunter could stretch his arms. Again, he tried to slow down. The stone chafed against his arms and legs, almost rubbing them raw.

He stopped trying and decided just to enjoy the ride.

How long he kept sliding, Hunter couldn't tell. Time meant nothing in the twilight under the earth. He could have been sliding for hours or days or even a week. He became tired and hungry. He drifted in and out of sleep. Always, his dimly lit surroundings looked the same: dark, rocky, wet.

He'd just drifted off once more when, suddenly, he woke with a jerk.

He wasn't in the slide tube anymore.

He was falling through some kind of huge underground cavern. He couldn't quite make out the walls, though their starlike illumination still sparkled faintly in the distance. The air of this new, vast space felt warm and moist.

Hunter tried yelling for help, but his voice came out a soft croak; he hadn't spoken for a long time. He didn't see any lava waiting below, but he didn't see anything else, either. How long could he fall like this?

Something brushed against his face, something soft and pliable. Then another something, against his arm this time. Then more all around him, as though he were falling through sticky cotton candy.

Hunter peered into the darkness. A strange, fuzzy netting

seemed to be wrapped around his whole body. He slowed as the netting bent beneath him. Gradually, he came to a stop.

Hunter sighed with relief. He looked around, happy to have stopped sliding and falling. Where was he?

The light in this place was very dim—little more than starlight on a clear summer night. Hunter could barely make out the pale netting supporting his body. The walls of the cavern receded into the distance. Only the vague, twinkling minerals gave him any hint that he was in a big, shaftlike cave at all.

He looked down. Pale green-yellow light drifted up from somewhere. Hunter couldn't be sure where the light came from. He didn't see a hole or exit below. The light looked like sunlight reflecting through leaves, not like the fiery lava he'd seen earlier. Maybe it was a way out.

"If I can reach the cave wall, I can climb down and get out of here," Hunter thought.

Cautiously, he tried to stand on the netting. The sticky strands gave slightly beneath him. He wobbled and nearly fell off the net. He decided to crawl rather than walk to the edge.

A soft sound drifted to his ears from above. Hunter looked toward it, peering into the dark shadows. Something moved, and a vague clicking, skittering noise echoed in the darkness. The sound made a shiver run down Hunter's spine.

Six reddish orbs appeared in the night-black sky.

Hunter's blood ran cold. He'd seen orbs like that before. They were *eyes*—huge spider eyes!

The eyes drew closer as the spider's huge bulk came into view. It was monstrous, nearly as big as an elephant, and dark as midnight. It crept across the netting toward Hunter.

Hunter suddenly realized that this wasn't a net he was trapped in—it was a gigantic spiderweb! He screamed and tore at the gummy strands. The web covered his body in a sticky cocoon. The immense spider drew closer. Hunter thrashed harder, clawing wildly at the webbing.

His fingers ripped through one of the web's big support lines. The line snapped. Hunter lurched toward empty air. As he fell, he grabbed one of the long web strands. His fingers wrapped around the line and held tight. He did his best Tarzan impression and swung toward the wall of the cave. He kept his eyes forward, not daring to look back.

The sounds of the giant spider approaching echoed behind him.

The wall drew into focus as Hunter swung toward it. He spotted a gap in the stone through which vague greenish light shone. Hunter aimed for the opening and prayed.

His web rope reached its limit a few yards short of the hole. Before the webbing could swing back, Hunter let go of it. He catapulted through the air into the opening. He didn't care what lay on the other side. Anything was better than a giant spider!

Hunter hit the slick surface of the new tube and tumbled downward. Water dripped on him from above, making the tube slippery, and he started sliding again. He braced himself for another wild ride.

Almost before he knew it, Hunter shot out the roof of a cavern so wide that he couldn't see its sides. For a moment, Hunter thought he'd fallen clear through the earth to the other side.

Some of the web covering his body snagged on the corner

of the opening. The sticky mesh stretched like a bungee cord, then broke. Hunter plunged through the air.

The jungle-covered ground rushed up toward him at a frightening rate. The shredded webbing trailed behind him like a parachute. It slowed him down slightly and snagged on a big branch when he hit the first tree.

Most of the branches in the treetop were thin and supple. They whipped past Hunter as he fell. The webbing on his body snagged the limbs and unraveled, slowing him down further. The leaves brushed his exposed arms and legs, stinging his skin. He shot through the branches and into something soft—more webbing! Before Hunter could even worry about that, the webbing broke.

He tumbled through more layers of tree branches and webs. Each layer sent a jolt through his body and up his spine as he cartwheeled from side to side. He rolled through a final shock of leaves and crashed to the ground.

Hunter lay on his belly, stunned and bruised. The world swirled around him. Every bone in his body ached. He fought back the pain and forced his eyes to focus.

He was lying on a beach of fine black sand. Whispering waves lapped against the shore.

Hunter sat up. Ahead of him a vast sea stretched into the distance. Behind him lay the edge of an immense green jungle.

A weird orange light played over the ocean's surface. Hunter thought he was seeing a sunset, though the sun was nowhere near the horizon. The trees of the jungle looked strange, too. They were tall and fernlike, resembling something in a book about dinosaurs. And was that a shipwreck he saw on the shore in the distance?

Hunter scratched his head. "Where am I?" he asked aloud. "Am I dreaming?" Being caught in the giant spider's web certainly seemed like a nightmare. Perhaps everything that had happened to him since falling into the sinkhole had been just a bad dream.

Yes, Hunter decided. That made sense. He had gotten hurt in the landslide and now lay dreaming in a hospital bed somewhere. He pinched himself to try to wake up.

"Ouch!"

The pinch hurt. Pinches weren't supposed to hurt in a dream, were they? But what if he *wasn't* sleeping...

A pang of worry twisted in Hunter's stomach. Had he really fallen through to the other side of the world? Or had he just fallen into an immense cavern inside the earth? Was he inside or outside?

He took a deep breath and looked up to check for any sign of the cave ceiling. What he saw made his stomach clench even more.

Above him loomed a huge praying mantis, at least twenty feet tall. The colossal bug gazed hungrily at Hunter as it lurched forward. Its armored mouth parts clicked, and a long string of saliva dripped from its fangs. The huge insect raised its hooklike claws, preparing to strike.

3
Spider Rider

"I shouldn't watch so many monster movies," Hunter told himself.

Then the bug lunged at him. Its monstrous claws slashed down. Instinctively, Hunter rolled out of the way.

One of the mantis's claws brushed Hunter's leg. The impact bruised his thigh, and Hunter yelped in pain.

"That hurt!" he cried. Dream or not, he decided not to stick around for any more.

Scrambling to his feet, he dodged out of the way as the mantis attacked again. The insect's claws slammed into the beach, spraying stinging black sand into the air.

Hunter shook the sand out of his eyes and ran. The bug stood between him and the beach, so he headed into the jungle. Huge trees that looked like ferns and giant palms arced overhead. Flowers with petals the size of dinner plates covered the forest floor. Hunter dodged through the underbrush, trying to find a spot too tight for the mantis to squeeze into.

The mantis rustled through the foliage after him, clicking its mandibles and making a screeching sound. Hunter hoped it wasn't communicating with others of its kind, telling them to ambush him as he ran. A thick stand of jungle ahead of him swayed, and Hunter skidded to a stop.

An enormous spider pushed through the leaves, right in front of him. Hunter estimated that the spider stood ten feet high at its shoulders, and he counted six blazing golden eyes. An armored carapace with sleek black hair like a tarantula's covered its body. Saplings and other small plants bent aside as the monster spider lurched forward. The arachnid's multiple eyes gleamed with predatory intelligence.

Hunter made a quick U-turn, not caring where he went, so long as he got away from the huge spider. He raced pell-mell through the jungle, heading back toward the shore, trying not to run into the mantis while he ran from the arachnid.

Sweat beaded on his body and poured down his forehead. He felt hot and scared and very tired. What was he doing here? Could this nightmare place be real?

This spider didn't look like the one whose web he'd been caught in before. How many of these monsters could there be? Neither spider looked like anything he'd ever seen on earth before—and Hunter knew all about spiders. And of course both spiders were much, much bigger than any he'd ever heard about.

Hunter remembered all the stories he'd read or seen where travelers got sucked through space-time wormholes into strange and distant lands. Had that happened to him?

The beach came into sight again through an opening in the jungle. He ran toward it, hoping to escape in the water from the giant bugs.

At the edge of the foliage, the giant mantis lurched out of the underbrush and cut him off. It swung a huge green claw at Hunter. He ducked but not quite enough.

The insect's big claw slammed into him. The space between the spines on the mantis's forelegs was just wide enough for Hunter's body to fit between, so he wasn't impaled.

But the limb still hit him hard. Hunter flew backward and crashed into a tree trunk at least five feet wide. The air rushed out of his lungs, and spots danced before his eyes.

The mantis swung again. Again Hunter ducked. This time the insect's giant claw flashed over his head, biting into the tree. A shower of splinters filled the air. Hunter staggered around the tree trunk, trying to put the tree between himself and the mantis.

The bug hissed and shrieked, pounding its sharp curved limbs into the tree, trying to catch Hunter. Hunter kept circling around the wide trunk, like a cartoon rabbit trying to outwit a hunter. The situation would have seemed comical if it hadn't been so deadly.

Hunter ducked another blow and circled one last time. He started to bolt deeper into the jungle, but the brush in front of him moved again. Another huge spider emerged from the foliage in front of him.

This wasn't either of the spiders he'd seen earlier. It was a sleeker, more colorful arachnid, though it was still nearly the size of an elephant. Hunter froze in his tracks, staring in amazement.

Standing on the back of the spider, riding it as though it were a huge surfboard, was a girl. She looked to be about Hunter's age or perhaps a little older. Hunter couldn't help noticing her colorful armorlike costume, with flared shoulders, gloves, and boots. A large silver bracelet covered with spider designs encircled her right wrist.

Hunter stood trapped with his back to the wide tree, caught between the mantis and the spider. Was the girl controlling these hideous insectoids? Was she the ruler of this place?

The girl's liquid eyes burned with hatred and cold determination.

Hunter knew that he was doomed. He tried again, in vain, to wake up.

The girl surged forward on her horrible beast, her eyes narrowed. She drew her spear and hoisted it to shoulder height. "Venus, attack!" she cried.

The spider rushed toward Hunter. He turned to flee, but the mantis rose up in front of him, its claws raised for the kill.

Hunter dived for the ground, knowing he could never avoid both monsters. The gigantic spider rushed right over him, not even slowing down. Hunter looked up, surprised to still be alive.

The spider and its rider crashed into the giant insect. The mantis turned to face them, bringing up its sharp, curved claws. The rider's lance glanced off the giant insect's left arm.

The mantis shrieked and whirled, its claws cutting through the air like curved swords.

The girl and her mount moved as one, leaping aside. The spider bounced off the trunk of the tree near Hunter and landed lightly on the ground behind the big green bug.

The girl stabbed at the creature with her lance. The mantis ducked aside, but not fast enough. Sparks flew as the spear hit the bug hard on the side of the head. The mantis toppled.

It flailed out with its legs as it fell. One of the slender green appendages knocked the lance from the girl's grip. Another limb connected hard with her spider.

The spider and rider went down, too, though the girl remained perched on the yellow-and-green arachnid's back.

The mantis regained its feet first. It raised its claws to attack.

Hunter didn't know exactly what was going on, but despite his fear of spiders, he wasn't about to let a human girl get killed by a giant insect.

He lunged forward and tackled the hindmost of the mantis's legs. He wrapped his arms around the bug's limb, which was thick as a young tree.

The mantis lurched forward, unbalanced by Hunter's added weight. The insect shook its leg hard. Hunter lost his grip and flew back, slamming into the tree trunk once more.

The girl and her spider scrambled to their feet, not noticing Hunter's heroic effort. She snatched up her lance.

She pointed her weapon at the big insect. "Lightning lance!" she cried. The silver bracelet on her wrist glowed, and a bolt of white electricity blasted out of the spear point.

The lightning seared through the air and slammed hard into the body of the giant mantis. The mantis shrieked and fell backward, stunned.

The girl and her spider leaped forward. Webs shot from the spider's body, entangling the downed insect. The spider worked quickly, manipulating the webs with its legs, weaving a silky cocoon around the dazed mantis.

The mantis struggled, cutting some of the webs with its hooked claws, but the girl and her mount proved too fast for it. In less than two minutes, the giant bug was completely wrapped.

Lying on the jungle floor, Hunter watched in amazement.

The girl laughed, a light, pleasant sound, and hopped off the back of her spider. She landed on the ground next to the helpless mantis and reached toward its head.

The bug continued to struggle. It snapped his jaws, but the girl remained out of reach.

She wrapped her fingers around a disklike node on the back of the mantis's neck. With a twist and a hard pull, she yanked the armored disk off the insect.

The mantis's body shook violently and became very pale. Its shell began to fade. The webs encircling the creature went slack as the whole, hideous monster turned into green mist. The girl held the chitinous disk high. The mist seeped into the glowing disk until nothing remained of the giant insect.

The disk went dark, and the girl tucked it into her belt. Then she pulled a small, gooey bundle from the webbing where the mantis had been. The bundle looked like a cocoon. Hunter realized that it had been attached to the creature's back. He'd been too busy fighting for his life to notice it at first.

The rider reached up, patted her spider on the side, and smiled. She pulled apart the strands of the cocoon, checked inside it, and tucked it into a roughly woven pack slung across her back. Then she turned toward Hunter and the smile faded from her face. Her gigantic spider turned toward him as well.

"Uh...hi," Hunter stammered. "Hey, thanks for saving me and all, but I probably should get going. I'm sure my parents are worried about me, and..."

The giant spider opened its deadly looking mandibles. A purple flash streaked out.

Something hit Hunter's neck. It felt like a bee sting. "Ouch!" Hunter cried, slapping his hand over the spot.

He rubbed his neck. The world swam around him.

"Hey...what did you...?" he began.

Before he could finish, he fell to the ground, unconscious.

4
Captive!

Hunter Steele woke not knowing where he was. He felt as if he were a piece of baggage being hauled around an airport terminal—jostled, bruised, and almost sick from all the bumping around.

He opened his eyes and found himself lying on his back, staring at the sky. Overhead, the jungle moved past quickly, as though he were riding in a car over a very bumpy woodland road.

Hunter tried to move and discovered he couldn't, not much anyway. Masses of sticky web ropes lashed him to the back of a giant spider, but he was just able to sit up. Hunter's stomach clenched with fear.

This was the same yellow-and-green spider that had battled the mantis in the jungle earlier. The girl warrior sat in front of Hunter, riding on the spider's back. The wind of their swift movement blew her blond hair backward. Her locks waved and dangled, like spider legs, over the tattered pack on her back.

Anger fought against the fear within Hunter's chest. He didn't like spiders much, but he also didn't like being tied up as if he were a criminal.

"Hey!" he called. "Hey, you!"

The girl turned her head and looked at him sternly. "Quiet, traitor," she said.

"Traitor?" Hunter replied. "What are you talking about?"

"Venus and I have decided that you must be the spy who was working with that mantis," the girl said. "No wonder the Insectors were able to penetrate our defenses."

"In case you hadn't noticed," Hunter said, "that mantis was trying to *kill* me. Also, I saved your life back there!"

The girl scoffed. "Saved my life?"

Hunter scowled at her. "I grabbed that bug's leg. That's why it stumbled. What did you think, it was just clumsy?"

"Venus says she didn't see you help, either," the girl replied.

"Who's this Venus?" Hunter asked. "I don't know anyone by that name. How can she claim to know me or what I've been doing? And who are *you*, for that matter?"

The girl frowned at him. "I am Corona, of the Spider Riders of Arachnia—not that it matters to you, traitor."

"I'm *not* a traitor or a spy," Hunter insisted. "I don't know what any of this is about. But I *did* try to help you in your fight against the mantis."

"Even if you did, it might have been a ploy," Corona replied, "so you could escape with—" She stopped midsentence.

"With what?" Hunter asked.

Her eyes narrowed. "As if you didn't know!"

"But I *don't* know!" he fumed.

Corona turned away.

"You're making a big mistake," Hunter insisted.

She ignored him as they moved swiftly down the forested shore. Hunter struggled to keep upright. Sitting on the back of a spider doing fifty miles an hour—as best Hunter could guess—was tricky.

The spider moved gracefully but tended to climb over

obstacles rather than go around them. Riding on spiderback felt like riding on an eight-legged all-terrain vehicle. If it hadn't been a spider, Hunter might have enjoyed the ride.

The girl, Corona, had no trouble maintaining her balance. She was seated astride the spider, just behind its legs, as though she were riding a horse. Hunter didn't see any reins and wondered how she controlled the spider without them.

He thought back to the fight earlier. He remembered Corona having her boots wedged into small, stirrup-like openings in the spider's armor. Those must have kept her upright. Still, it seemed a tricky job at best.

Hunter figured she must have had a lot of practice riding on spiderback. Maybe it was as normal to her people as riding a bicycle was back home. For a moment, he wondered how long it had taken her to learn. He'd learned to snowboard one weekend and had hardly ever fallen after that.

For a moment, Hunter got caught up in thinking about how thrilling it must be to ride like Corona. Then he remembered, this was a *spider* they were riding on. An involuntary shudder ran down his spine.

To take his mind off the spider, Hunter decided to figure out which way they were headed. He looked for the sun, figuring that would help him tell east from west.

The sun looked strange, larger than he'd ever seen it before. It looked redder, too, even redder than sunset back home. It was too high in the sky to be sunset, though. The molten orb hung in the humid air ahead of them and to his right.

Suddenly, Hunter realized why it looked so different. The "sun" was imbedded in the ceiling of a cavern so immense that it encompassed all the land as far as he could see. The world of the spiders arched up around him like the inside of a huge upside-down bowl. He wasn't looking at the sun at all! He was gazing at the molten core of the earth!

Hunter's mouth dropped open. "Where *are* we?" he asked, awestruck.

Corona, who had ignored him for most of the ride, turned and replied. "On the shore of the Great Sea."

"Well, where's that?"

She gave him a funny look. "In Arachnia, far from the great city plateau—if that's what you mean."

"Maybe," Hunter said. "But I don't know where Arachnia is, either."

"Funny for a spy not to know where he is," Corona said.

"I told you," Hunter said, "I'm *not* a spy. I'm not even from this world."

Now she looked a bit concerned. "What do you mean?" she asked.

"Well, we're in the center of the earth, right?" he asked.

"Of course," she said. "Any idiot knows that."

"I don't, because I'm not from down here," Hunter said. "I fell through this hole, and—"

"I've heard enough of your lies," Corona said, turning away once more. "Our prince will determine what to do with you once we reach the city."

Hunter tried to get her attention again, but she ignored him. So, he occupied his time by trying to wriggle free of his bonds while watching the scenery go by.

They rambled down the black sand shore, past the ruins of the ancient ship he'd spotted earlier. To Hunter, the wreck looked like something out of a history book. He tried to ask Corona about it, but she still wasn't talking to him.

Ahead of them, another Spider Rider appeared. He rode

out of the trees, moving quickly, and headed straight for Hunter and Corona.

Hunter wondered for a moment if Corona and this new rider might fight. But the two fell in alongside each other, as though they were old friends.

The new rider was an older teen. Form-fitting armor, like the shell of a crab, covered his slender body. He rode a large, massive spider, with colorful red markings. The teenager smiled at Corona as he spoke. "I'm glad you accomplished our mission," he said, as though continuing an old conversation. "I caught my quarry, too. But he didn't have the prize. I had begun to worry." He eyed the roughly woven pack on Corona's back and smiled.

"We were lucky, Igneous," Corona replied. "Mantid's agents could have easily slipped through our fingers. Then our city, and perhaps the whole kingdom, would have been doomed."

"Hopefully, the other riders the prince sent out have discovered something useful," Igneous said. "I don't know how long we can last without the—" He stopped suddenly, as if someone had cut him off, though no one had said anything.

"Is this the spy you caught?" he asked, looking at Hunter.

"We're not sure," Corona replied. "We found him with the mantis. It's possible he's an Insector agent."

Igneous nodded. "Venus told Flame something like that as I was leaving the jungle."

"Excuse me!" Hunter said angrily. At first, the presence of another huge spider had frightened him. Now, though, he felt mad at being caught up in something he didn't understand. These people were speaking as though he wasn't even there!

"I am *not* a spy," he said. "I've been trying to tell you that. I'm not even from this world. I fell down here from the world above—from the surface of the earth."

Both spiders came to a sudden halt.

"What?" Corona asked, incredulous.

"I said I'm from the surface," Hunter replied. "I fell through a hole and ended up here. I don't know exactly where here is, but ... "

The spiders, Corona, and Igneous looked at one another with a series of quick glances. Hunter got the feeling they were having some kind of silent conversation.

"That's impossible," Igneous finally said.

"Well, I would have thought so, too," Hunter said, "but here I am. I am definitely *not* from Arachnia, I am definitely *not* a spy, and I have no idea what you're both going on about."

Corona looked at Igneous.

He shook his head. "Don't even think it," Igneous said. "It's some kind of trick."

"But, Igneous," she said, "he could be the one in the prophecy!"

5
Land of the Spiders

Igneous scoffed. "Our people have always talked about the prophecy of the Earthen," he said. "I, for one, don't believe it." He looked at his spider. "Flame doesn't believe it, either."

"But no one from the upper world has arrived in Arachnia since you and I were born," Corona said.

Igneous crossed his sinewy arms over his chest. "And this kid's not the first. It's as you said: he's working with Mantid and his Insectors."

"Okay, first," Hunter said, "my name is Hunter—Hunter Steele—not 'kid.' Second, I *am* from the upper world, whether you believe me or not. Third, I don't know who Mantid is or what an Insector is."

Corona rubbed her chin thoughtfully. "Hunter Steele...," she said. "It is a good name. A strong name." She looked as though she was reevaluating Hunter and his situation.

"So, now you can tell spies by their names, Corona?" Igneous asked. "As you said, he was associating with the mantis."

"If by 'associating,'" Hunter put in, "you mean nearly getting killed while I was trying to help Corona fight that bug—well, yeah, then I guess you could say I was 'associating.'" He tried to cross his arms over his chest, but the sticky web ropes prevented him from doing so.

Igneous ignored him and continued. "It doesn't matter

what his name is, Corona," the older teen said, "or even if his absurd claim about being Earthen is true. It's for Prince Lumen to decide whether he's a spy—not us."

"Yes," Corona said. "I agree, of course, as does Venus. Lumen is our leader; he will have the final say."

"Also, remember," Igneous continued, "the prophecy says that the arrival of an Earthen will cause upheaval in Arachnia. His coming will herald terrible war with the Insectors. If this boy *is* from the surface world"—he hooked his thumb toward Hunter—"a lot of Turandot could get killed."

"What's a Turandot?" Hunter asked.

"Our people," Corona told him. "We humans of the Inner World call ourselves the Turandot." She turned back to Igneous and nodded grimly. "You're right. We're wasting time here. Lumen will decide."

Igneous nodded. "We four are in agreement then?" he said. No one replied, but the spiders and their riders turned and galloped off once more.

"What four?" Hunter asked. But again, the riders paid him no attention. They kept heading in the direction Hunter had decided to call south.

They reached the end of the ocean, crossed a spur of jungle, and then entered a desolate, rocky area.

They passed small, smoking geysers and deep cracks in the ground. The smaller fissures the spiders merely stepped over. The larger ones they leaped. Hunter nearly lost his stomach on several of the jumps.

They came to a series of huge waterfalls. The strange thing was, the falls didn't fall down, they fell *up*, from the cavern floor toward the rocky ceiling, almost invisible high above. Hunter couldn't figure out what trick of gravity caused this weird phenomenon. Maybe being so close to the center of the earth distorted gravity somehow. However they worked, the falls were extraordinarily beautiful.

"What are those?" Hunter asked, pointing.

"Falls from Below," Corona answered curtly.

"How do they work?"

"No one knows," Igneous replied. "Even a spy should know that."

Eventually, they left the blasted plains and reached the shore of a huge lake. They began to see people now, just a few at first in lonely homes, then tiny communities.

The riders and their prisoner sped past small fishing villages and tiny farm towns. Hunter spotted several other Spider Riders as they went—all sitting on the backs of monstrous arachnids.

He noticed something strange: all the riders were young, or at least not full-grown adults. Adults and smaller kids worked the fields, tended the nets, and performed other work. But he saw no grown-up Spider Riders.

The society looked primitive to Hunter. He saw no paved highways or cars. Carts pulled by giant domesticated aphids dotted the muddy pathways that served as roads. Hunter saw no street signs, billboards, or electric lights or fast-food restaurants or anything that would have been commonplace in nearly any town in the surface world.

Yet the people seemed happy going about their business, dressed in their simple silken outfits. The workers waved when they saw the Spider Riders. Corona and Igneous waved back. Hunter got the impression that the riders were kind of like the knights of old—protecting the Turandot from Insectors, whatever those might be.

"Um, Ms. Corona," he said, trying to catch her attention, "was the big mantis thing you saved me from an Insector?"

"Of course," Corona replied.

"And you protect these people from the Insectors?"

"Among other things," she said.

"Well, you protected me from an Insector, so I must be an ordinary guy like these folks," Hunter concluded.

"Very clever," Igneous sneered.

Hunter fumed. He didn't know the older rider had been listening. He changed the subject. "So, did you people come down here in that old boat I saw by the side of the ocean?"

"Not us," Corona said. "But our ancestors did. That is all that remains of the First Transport."

"Others have come to the Inner World," Igneous added, "by different routes."

"Well, I didn't want to come," Hunter said. "So, if it's okay with you, I'll go back home. You can just cut me loose from these web ropes and I'll be on my way."

"No one ever returns to the surface," Igneous said grimly. "No one has ever found the way."

"At least, not since the early days of our people," Corona corrected him.

"That Arachna-Master is just legend," Igneous said. "Those who come to Arachnia stay here."

"Some people consider Earthen to be legendary as well," Corona said. She glanced at Hunter.

Igneous regarded the boy suspiciously. "There's a better chance that he's a spy than a true Earthen," he said.

The Spider Riders set a course along the shore of the huge lake. A series of huge plateaus, steep-sided flat-topped hills, sprang up out of the forest ahead of them. On the largest and most distant plateau sat an immense building complex. Peering through the haze, Hunter couldn't be sure exactly what it was. It looked like a huge fortress city, many miles away. The Spider Riders seemed to be heading toward it as they skirted the edge of the lake.

Although the riders didn't speak to him much, Corona did reach back from time to time to give Hunter water. He drank from a canteen shaped like the body of a crab spider that Corona kept strapped to the back of her mount.

They rode along the lakeshore until they ran into a large river. They followed it upstream, riding between it and the forest, heading toward one of the smaller plateaus.

As they went, Hunter managed to work his hands loose from the webs. Neither Corona nor Igneous seemed too worried about his newfound freedom. Hunter's legs remained stuck fast. Even if they hadn't been, Hunter couldn't really go anywhere. Riding on the back of a giant spider was dangerous enough; jumping off a speeding arachnid seemed completely foolhardy. So, Hunter fought down his fears and waited to see what would happen.

"Are we going to the city on the plateau?" he asked the next time Corona gave him a drink.

"Yes," she replied. "To Arachnia."

"I thought the world was called Arachnia."

"Both world and city," she said. She didn't glare at Hunter as much as she had when they'd first met. He wondered if Corona might be starting to believe that he *had* come from the surface world. Somehow, that made Hunter feel a little bit better—though he still hated riding on the back of a giant spider.

Since the riders clearly weren't about to release him, he

tried to get comfortable. The webbing and his precarious position on spiderback made this difficult.

Hunter's legs already felt numb. How long had he been in this weird place, anyway? It seemed like ages. He checked the "sun," hoping to see how far it had moved since he first arrived. The glowing red-orange orb still hung in the same spot in the sky.

"Um, Corona," Hunter said, "does the sun ever move here? We've been traveling for hours, and it hasn't changed at all."

"Why would the sun change?" Corona asked. "It is the one constant of the Inner World. All things change, save the sun."

"Where I come from, sometimes there isn't even a sun in the sky at all," Hunter added. "Then it gets dark. We call that nighttime. It's when we sleep."

"Here we sleep when we are tired," Corona said. "And we cover our sleeping quarters with drapes. It is easier to sleep in the dark."

"So, the sun never sets here?" Hunter said.

"Never," Igneous replied.

"And it never gets dark?"

"Only inside, with the curtains drawn," Corona said. "Or underground."

Hunter wiped the sweat from his forehead. "No wonder it's so hot."

"Today is rather cool, actually," Corona said, "because the wind blows from over the distant sea."

"Hold!" Igneous commanded. His spider pulled up short on a small bluff by the riverside.

"What is it?" Corona asked. Then added, "Quiet, Venus. I can't hear through you and Flame chattering."

Hunter felt puzzled. He didn't hear anything.

They'd grown very near one of the small plateaus now, and Hunter could make out signs of human construction atop the rocky outcropping. A beautiful waterfall cascaded down the cliff face. This waterfall ran normally, top to bottom, like the waterfalls Hunter was used to. The falls fell into the river that Hunter and the riders had been following.

On the far side of the river lay a medium-size town with thatched-roof houses. Farmers labored in irrigated fields on both sides of the river. Fishermen worked the riverbanks, as well. A small ferry, perhaps big enough for two aphid-drawn carts, stood on the village side of the river. The town looked like a peaceful, pleasant place.

Igneous pointed to a spot in the forest ahead and to their left—between them and the town. There they saw a large blackened clearing, the size of several soccer fields, amid the greenery. Hunter guessed that a recent forest fire must have destroyed the trees. The clearing wouldn't have been visible to them at all if they hadn't been atop the riverside bluff. The forest completely blocked the view from the river, from the plateau ahead, and from the town beyond.

"Yes, I see them," Corona said, apparently talking to no one.

"See what?" Hunter asked.

She pointed toward the edge of the clearing.

Hunter's eyes grew wide as a giant insectoid stepped from the greenery and scuttled into the forest on the far side. Another followed, then another and another, all moving quickly, as though trying to hide their presence. Some kept to the edges of the clearing, while others dashed quickly across the blackened expanse. The creatures looked like monstrous humanoid centipedes. They carried spears and swords and other weapons of war.

A chill of realization shot down Hunter's spine: a huge army of giant insects was moving stealthily through the forest, preparing to attack the unsuspecting town.

6
Riders to the Rescue

"Are those Insectors?" Hunter asked.

"Of course," Igneous replied.

"But they look like centipede-men," Hunter said, "not praying mantises."

"They are Centipedians," Corona said.

"There's more than one kind of Insector?" Hunter asked.

"There are many kinds," Corona replied. "Mantises, the Cockroach People, Snowmites, and Centipedians—'pedes, we call them—among many others."

"So there are Insector ants, bees, that kind of thing?" Hunter asked.

"Not all giant insects interfere with humans," Corona said. "Some go about their business peacefully. Many did so...until Mantid came to power."

"Who's Mantid?" Hunter asked.

"You're overplaying your ignorance, kid," Igneous said. He shot Hunter a knowing frown. "Now keep silent. We won't have you alerting your Insector comrades to our presence."

"But—" Hunter began. Igneous's reddish spider glared at him. Hunter shut up.

Hunter felt frustrated. Apparently, Igneous thought he was merely pretending not to know things about this world. How would Hunter ever get the Spider Riders to trust him? Did he even want their trust?

Igneous and Corona and their spiders exchanged glances. Were they giving one another signals? Hunter didn't see any hand signs or other obvious means of silent communication.

After a moment, Igneous shook his head. "Flame still can't get through to Arachnia," he said. "Ebony isn't responding."

Now Hunter was really puzzled. Did Igneous have some kind of radio device with which to communicate with the Spider Rider city? Hunter didn't see any, and such technology seemed beyond the scientific knowledge of the Inner World.

"Venus says she's getting something vague from the town," Corona said. "She senses a familiar presence but not one of us. We four will have to go it alone."

Four? Hunter wondered again. He puzzled about the math for a moment—Corona plus Igneous made only two. Even if they counted Hunter on their side, which they didn't seem to, that made only three—not four. Which meant . . .

"Are *Flame* and *Venus* the names of your spiders?" Hunter blurted.

"Of course," Corona replied.

"I told you to stay quiet, kid," Igneous snapped. "Corona, you ride to Arachnia and bring help."

"But, Igneous," she replied, "the city is too far away. You won't be able to hold the Centipedians off that long."

"I'll have to," Igneous said. "What other choice do we have?"

"I can ride into battle with you," she said. "Together, we can last longer. And perhaps the watchers in Arachnia will see the conflict and send help."

Igneous looked to the distant city. "It's a long way to notice a fight," he said. "Especially with this haze hanging in the air."

"Not if the battle is big enough," Corona replied, smiling.

"Excuse me," Hunter put in. "If you two are getting into a fight, could you let me off here?"

Igneous's eyes narrowed. "Flame says freeing a spy before a battle would be very foolish," he said. "I agree."

Corona and her spider nodded as well.

"Terrific!" Hunter said, meaning just the opposite. "So what am *I* supposed to do?"

"Hang on," Corona replied. With that, she and Igneous and their spiders leaped forward and galloped top-speed toward the doomed town. Hunter's stomach lurched violently as they took off.

They sped down the bluff and along the river shore toward the city. As they did, the Centipedian army emerged from the forest into the irrigated fields across the river from the town. The Centipedians stood slightly taller than men and walked upright. Shell-like armor covered the Insectors' segmented bodies. Glowing antennae twitched atop their heads. They raised their weapons—spears, bows, and swords with rough-toothed blades.

Though the river stood between the Insectors and the town, the water looked like scant defense to Hunter.

As the Centipedians reached the riverbank, a man spotted them. He raced up a wooden tower near the riverside and began banging on a big metal plate.

"The warning gong," Corona said. "At least the town knows they're coming. They'll never hear the gong in Arachnia, though."

The Centipedians slung flaming balls of oil-soaked grass at the tower. The fireballs missed the signaler but quickly set the tower ablaze. The man dived into the river as the tower fell, burning. The water smothered the gong's final cry. Steam rose from the skeletal timbers of the lookout post as they sizzled into the cool liquid.

The town militia, armed with spears and other weapons, raced out to face the giant bugs. The Centipedians drew segmented metal shields from their backs and arranged them like a wall.

"The 'pedes are getting smarter!" Igneous said.

Corona nodded grimly. "Yes, every time we face them. They've never dared attack so close to the capital before."

"Until recently, we would have known they were coming," Igneous noted. "Our defenses have been compromised since..." He let the sentence trail off.

"Can our weapons pierce that shield wall?" Corona asked.

"We have to try," Igneous replied. "With luck we can catch the enemy from behind, before they turn their shield toward us."

The riders stood less than a mile away from the enemy now, and the bug army still hadn't seen them. The 'pedes dragged logs and vines from the jungle, putting all their energy into crossing the river. They formed their ragtag materials into a long makeshift bridge.

Arrows from the town militia rained down on the bugs. The Centipedian shield deflected most of the missiles. At the head of the bug army stood a Centipedian in red armor. He rode on the back of a titanic red scorpion and brandished a long, curve-bladed spear. The Insector leader waved his arms, gesturing orders to his troops. The antennae atop his head glowed brightly. Several Centipedian lieutenants scampered about, relaying the chief's commands.

The villagers formed a blockade on the town side of the

river, trying to cut off the invaders' makeshift bridge. The farmers had already fled from their fields on both sides of the river. Fishermen's nets lay abandoned by the waterside.

The Centipedian leader rose up on the back of his scorpion mount. His antennae flared and a blast of greenish energy flashed across the river. The energy bolt struck the front of the militia blockade. The people it hit crashed to the ground and lay unconscious. The whole human defensive formation fell back.

The bugs rammed their bridge over the water and began to swarm across.

Then a thunderous war whoop shook the air. "HIZZ-AHHH!"

The Insectors froze, startled by the cry.

A rider on the back of a sleek brown spider skittered down from the waterfall bluff. He landed behind the line of the Centipedians and lit into them with his lance. The startled bugs fell back. Their makeshift bridge crashed into the river.

"Magma and Brutus!" Corona said. "They were the presence Venus sensed!"

Igneous nodded. "Thank the Oracle that mercenary's still on our side. I only hope he hasn't ruined our—"

The older teen didn't finish the sentence. Even as he spoke, the Centipedians turned on Magma and his spider. As they did, they spotted Corona, Igneous, and Hunter.

"There goes our element of surprise," Corona said. "Magma always was too cocky for his own good."

"Or the good of *all* of us, in this case," Igneous added. "Too late to do anything about it now. As Magma said, 'HIZZ-AHHH!'" He spurred Flame forward and shot into the rear of the Centipedian army. Corona and Venus followed.

Hunter clung to the back of Corona's spider. He saw no good way to escape the coming battle.

"What have I gotten myself into?" he wondered.

7
Into the Fire

"I repeat," Hunter shouted, "you can let me off here!"

Igneous and Corona ignored him. They raised their right arms in unison. The manacle bracelets on their wrists glowed with white light.

"Lightning lance!" Corona cried.

"Fire bolt!" Igneous bellowed.

Blazing energy shot out of their weapons toward the Centipedians. Igneous's fiery shot bowled over a half-dozen of their enemies. Corona's bolt smashed against the Centipedian shield wall, bursting into brilliant but harmless sparks.

The sudden attack by three Spider Riders confused the bug army. The massed Centipedians fragmented into smaller, bewildered groups. Some turned to face Corona, Igneous, and Magma. Others continued trying to bridge the river. Still others milled around, unsure of what to do or where to turn.

The Centipedian commander shouted orders, but his Insectors didn't seem to be listening to him. He turned toward the riders and his antenna glowed.

"Shields!" Corona cried.

All three Spider Riders raised their arms, and chitinous shields radiated out of their manacles.

At the same time, the three spiders—Venus, Flame, and Brutus—scattered, giving the Insector leader no single target to focus on. Green energy blasted from the Centipedian commander toward Magma, who was the closest. Magma raised his shield as Brutus flattened his eight legs.

Most of the blast sailed over their heads. What little remained bounced off Magma's shield. The deadly energy burst like fireworks in the air.

That gave Hunter an idea. "Corona!" he called. "Why don't you use an energy bolt, like a flare, to alert the human army in the main city!"

Corona fended off a Centipedian with her lance, knocking the bug soldier flat. Venus shot a cord of web at the falling Insector, pinning it to the ground. "None of us has the signal flare power," Corona shouted back. "Our weapon bolts are not designed for that. They would not be strong enough to be seen at such a distance."

"But if you combined them, it might work—*urp*!"

The last word came out as kind of a queasy burp. Hunter's stomach didn't like Venus's lurching and jumping as she battled the bugs. He fought down the nausea and looked around. Though Igneous and Magma were fighting fairly close by, neither of them was within shouting distance. The clash of weapons and the stomping of bug feet made too much noise.

Corona nodded at Hunter. "It's worth a try," she said. She closed her eyes and concentrated a moment. As she did, Venus leaped over three 'pedes who were trying to skewer them with spears. One of the weapons glanced off the spider's side and jabbed into the webbing holding Hunter.

Hunter grabbed the shaft of the spear and pulled it out of the bug's grasp. He used the spear point to cut through the remaining webs that held his legs.

As Venus fended off two more Centipedians, Corona raised her manacle bracelet toward the sky. Without any word from her, Igneous and Magma did the same.

Simultaneously, all three riders shot energy bolts high into the air over the lake. The bursts crashed together, forming a spectacular display of light.

"Great job!" Hunter shouted. He wondered how they'd coordinated the feat. Again, he hadn't seen any obvious signals among them.

The Centipedian commander shrieked one final command at the 'pedes facing the riders, then turned back to building the bridge. At the command, the bug army's resolve firmed. The Insectors milling around returned to their ranks. Those facing the riders charged forward with renewed courage.

Slowly, the Insector bridge began coming together once more. But with the leader focusing on that task, he couldn't blast the Spider Riders again. So the three riders formed up next to one another and fought side by side.

The speed and agility of the Turandot spiders amazed Hunter. They seemed capable of fighting with all eight legs and their mandibles at the same time. They also possessed powers that he didn't understand.

Four times, Hunter saw purplish barbs flash from spider mouths. Each time, the Insectors hit by the darts fell senseless.

"That must be the same sting they used on me," Hunter thought.

The sleep sting didn't seem to be the spiders' main weapon, though. Usually they fought with claw and fang. Corona and the other riders mostly used their lances. Occasionally, one would fire an energy blast to thin out the bug opposition.

Hunter held tight to the back of Corona's spider. "The riders are powerful," he thought, "but they can't use their energy weapons all the time—just as the spiders can't sting endlessly."

A Centipedian that Corona didn't see charged toward them. Hunter raised the spear he'd captured and stabbed at the creature.

With one hand, the 'pede grabbed the weapon and pulled, nearly yanking Hunter off Venus. With the sword in its other hand, the creature swung at Corona's unprotected back.

Corona whirled at the last second and parried the blow. The 'pede yanked the spear out of Hunter's hand. He flipped it around and hurled it at Corona.

A round shield formed around Corona's spidery bracelet. The spear bounced harmlessly off it. She smashed her lance into the 'pede, and it went down.

Corona glared at Hunter. "I was lucky to spot that 'pede," she said. "Why didn't you warn me?"

"I was trying to help," he replied sheepishly.

"Just because you had *one* good idea, it doesn't make you a Spider Rider," she replied.

She turned back to the battle, leaving Hunter to brood.

All he could do now was hang on for dear life and try not to get killed by a stray Centipedian attack. Corona and the others did well enough without his help.

The Insectors fell back and re-formed their metal shield wall. The riders darted forward, their spiders spraying webbing across the metal surface. The webs stuck the shields to the ground, making it hard for the bugs to move.

Corona, Igneous, and Magma retreated slightly. All three panted hard to catch their breaths. Sweat drenched their armored bodies.

"The webs will buy us a brief rest," Igneous said. "Glad you could join us, Magma."

Magma, a muscular dark-haired boy about the same age as Igneous, nodded. "It wouldn't help my reputation if the town I was hired to guard got wiped out by Insectors."

Corona frowned. "Guarding a town this close to Arachnia city was probably a pretty cushy job until recently."

Magma frowned back at her. "Not as easy as you'd think," he said. "Though this is definitely the worst day I've had so far. Who's the kid, by the way?"

"A spy," Igneous began.

"An Earthen," Corona said simultaneously.

"I'm Hunter Steele," Hunter said. "I'm—"

Igneous cut him off. "Time for long introductions later," he said, "assuming we live through this." He looked at the 'pedes, who had nearly gnawed their way through the webbing holding them back.

"Corona," Igneous said, "you and Venus scale that bluff. Get in front of the 'pedes crossing the river and start a second front. With luck, we can catch them between us and break their spirit. Magma and I will stay here."

"You're sending her instead of me?" Magma asked. "Why? It's *my* town."

Igneous gave him a sly smile. "Because I know Corona and Venus will carry out my orders."

"Are you suggesting I'm unreliable?" Magma asked hotly.

"Just untrained," Igneous replied.

"Untrained!" Magma said. "I've fought more Insectors than you can even imagine! I live where the tough jobs are, not in some palace."

"Untrained in terms of coordinating with other riders, I

meant," Igneous corrected. Then to Corona, he added, "Take the outsider with you. See he stays out of trouble."

"I'd be happy to go home," Hunter offered.

"Or back to your Insector masters, more likely," Igneous said.

"I'll make sure he doesn't interfere," Corona said. Venus turned so quickly that Hunter nearly fell off the spider's back.

As they darted toward the sheer bluff face, the 'pede army broke through the webs and advanced toward Magma and Igneous. The two male riders and their spiders leaped forward, taking the battle to the enemy.

Hunter clung to Venus's back as they raced toward the sheer wall. For a moment, he wondered how they were going to get around the cliff. The next second, he knew as the gigantic spider ran straight up the rock.

The huge arachnid's legs clung easily to the rough stone. Corona remained standing, exquisitely balanced, on the spider's back.

Hunter gripped the remains of his web bonds until his knuckles went white. His feet dangled precariously in the air. He didn't dare to look down as the ground fell away beneath them. "This is what it must feel like going backward up the first drop of a roller coaster!" he thought.

Despite the thrill-ride aspect, Hunter didn't like it. His heart pounded in his ears. He clung desperately to the tattered webbing, wishing now that he hadn't cut himself free. Only a few sticky strands stood between him and a hundred-foot fall to his death.

Just when Hunter felt as though he couldn't hang on any longer, they reached the top of the cliff. Venus lurched to a stop. Hunter gasped with relief and flexed his aching hands. Corona looked around, surveying the situation.

Ahead of them lay a huge, man-made dam holding back a sizeable reservoir. The spillway at the dam's far edge created the waterfall Hunter had seen from below. The water cascaded over the precipice and down to the river running past the town.

The plateau, which looked small from the village side, actually stretched away into a large highland area and into tall, distant hills. Beyond the cliff-top lake lay more irrigated farms.

Cautiously, because of the slippery wet rock, Venus edged around the front side of the dam. The spider reached the spillway and leaped over it, landing deftly on the far side.

"This is as far as you go," Corona said to Hunter.

"What?" Hunter replied. After clinging to the spider's back for so long, he could hardly believe his ears.

A few minutes ago, he'd wanted to get out of the battle and as far away from the riders and their hideous mounts as he could. However, being stranded, alone, at the top of a bluff in an alien world...Hunter didn't want that, either. "But—" he began.

"I won't carry you with me into this battle," Corona continued. "I'm not sure if you're really Earthen, but I'm fairly sure you're *not* a spy—despite what happened earlier. I'd hate to have you accidentally killed in the fighting."

"I'm all for not getting killed," Hunter said. "But am I really safe up here?" He looked over the cliff to where the riders and villagers battled the Centipedians below. "Maybe I could help you somehow," he said. Hunter didn't want the humans in this place slaughtered by the bugs—even if the Turandot *were* friends with the horrible spiders.

"Are you trained as a warrior?" Corona asked. "Your spear work wasn't very good. It nearly cost me my life."

"I've beaten the Hive Level on Alien Smash Four," Hunter said.

Corona looked puzzled. "I've never heard of this battlefield Alien Smash," she said. "Where is it?"

"It's..." Hunter began. Then he considered what he'd been about to say. Being a master of video games probably didn't *really* count as battle experience. "It's this game, see..."

"Ah. Something like a practice joust."

"Well, no. Not exactly," Hunter said. He sighed. "I guess when you come down to it, I'm not *really* a warrior." Not wanting to appear completely foolish, he added, "I haven't finished my training."

"Then wait here," Corona ordered. "There will be time enough to complete your training after this battle." She gave him a shove off the back of her giant spider. Hunter stumbled and nearly fell on his face as he landed on the shore of the reservoir. Corona and Venus crawled over the precipice and down the cliff.

Hunter admired the warrior girl's poise and balance. The Spider Rider never wavered as her spider scampered down the vertical cliff face. The pack containing the cocoon she'd recovered from the mantis earlier stayed securely on Corona's back.

Hunter had spent a lot of time snowboarding back home. He'd gotten good enough at it to do some complex tricks. Riding on the back of a giant spider looked even more difficult. Hunter wondered how long it took to master spider riding.

Corona and Venus quickly reached the base of the cliff below the dam. They circled around, concealing themselves behind the village's outlying buildings, hoping to catch the advancing Centipedians by surprise.

The evil bugs had finally bridged the river. They swarmed across the makeshift span and battled toe-to-toe with the brave villagers. The bugs and the humans seemed fairly well matched in weaponry, save for the occasional antenna blast from the 'pede leader. The Turandot were badly outnumbered, though.

Magma and Igneous, fighting in the farm fields between the forest and the riverside, stood surrounded by their enemies. Both riders fought savagely with their lances, felling many of their foes. The 'pedes kept swarming in from the forest. No matter how many of them the riders knocked down, more Insectors came to fill the gaps.

Suddenly, Corona burst from concealment. She rode Venus hard into the side of the Centipedians' advancing line.

Her sudden attack startled the bugs. Many of them fell back toward their makeshift bridge. More than a dozen actually fell into the river and were swept downstream toward the distant lake. The leader of the 'pedes, standing near the far edge of the bridge, seemed confused. He blasted at Corona with his antennae, but his shots missed her.

Hunter smiled. It looked as though Igneous's plan was working. By starting another battlefront, the riders might be able to break the bugs' spirit and drive them back into the forest. Hunter's heart swelled with the thrill of the humans' impending victory.

Then he noticed something the Spider Riders hadn't: a section of 'pedes had broken off from the main group. While Corona and the villagers battled to drive the bugs back into the river, this new group sneaked through the town, away from the battle.

For a moment, this puzzled Hunter. Then he realized that the 'pedes meant to attack Corona from behind—just as she had surprised them moments earlier.

"Corona!" Hunter shouted, trying to warn her. But she was much too far away to hear. He jumped up and down and waved his hands, trying to get her attention. It was no use. None of the riders was looking in his direction.

Hunter wished that he had an energy blast like theirs, to use as a warning flare. He didn't, though. Determination to save the riders, make up for his mistakes, and find his way home rose up inside him. He could think of only one thing to do.

Taking a deep breath to steady himself, Hunter Steele climbed down the cliff face toward the battle.

8
Trapped Between Fire and Water

Hunter moved down the rocks as quickly as he could. He was determined to help Corona, to make up for what had happened earlier. Ten feet above the ground, his grip gave way and he fell. He landed hard on the riverbank, and the air rushed out of his lungs.

"Oof!"

He picked himself up and sprinted between the outlying buildings, heading for the main village. The Spider Riders continued to fight the Centipedian army on the small, irrigated farms flanking both riverbanks. The bugs that had crossed the bridge tried to push out of the farmland into the town, but Corona and the town militia held them back.

On the opposite side of the river, Magma and Igneous harassed the bug army's rear ranks. Irrigation ditches running out from the river slowed down the bugs, whose legs were not made to deal with such obstacles. The Turandot spiders stepped nimbly between the ruts. A few farmers slogged through the mud as well, fighting to protect their homes. The Turandot villagers fought bravely, but the bug army was too large to hold back for long. Only the narrowness of the makeshift bridge kept the town from being overwhelmed.

While climbing down the cliff, Hunter had looked for any sign of help from Arachnia city. He'd been unable to see any reinforcements through the haze, though.

Hidden from Corona's view by the fighting and the outlying buildings, the small band of sneaky Centipedians crept toward the Spider Rider's exposed back.

Hunter ran as fast as he could, wanting to help Corona. He cut between a waterside mill and a drying shed, picking the most direct course. He rounded the corner of the mill, shouting again to warn her. "Corona!"

But he'd miscalculated. She wasn't within sight. More buildings lay ahead of him. At street level, the village was much more confusing than when he'd looked down on it from atop the cliff. "Am I even running in the right direction?" Hunter wondered.

In front of him a Centipedian stepped around a building. The creature stood half again as tall as Hunter. Shell-like armor covered its brutish body. Its segmented form looked vaguely human but also hideously insectlike. The antennae on top of the 'pede's skull twitched as the bug saw Hunter.

The creature swung its metal-tipped club toward Hunter's head. He ducked under the blow and kept running. The Centipedian turned, hissing, and gave chase.

Hunter wished he had some kind of weapon to fight the bug, but he didn't. So, he figured the best thing to do was just keep running to try to warn Corona about the ambush.

Hunter and the Insector passed between storage sheds and outbuildings as they ran. The bug chittered and hissed, calling to its comrades. Two more bugs left the sneak attack group and chased after Hunter.

Hunter cut back toward the river, hoping the Insectors might bog down in the muddy farmland. The irrigation ruts slowed them just enough, and he escaped back between the buildings.

Hunter scampered up a mill's waterwheel to get a better view and figure out where he was. The big wheel was like a slippery moving staircase. Hunter kept his balance and quickly reached the top.

On the other side of the mill, he spotted Corona battling the main bug army. She didn't see the Insectors sneaking up behind her.

"Corona!" Hunter shouted. He skidded down the far side of the waterwheel and ran toward the Spider Rider.

The bug ambush party rushed forward, looking to stab Corona with their spears.

"Corona!" She still didn't hear him.

An uncoiled rope lay on the ground between Corona and the bugs. Rumpled wet sheets and clothing were draped over the cord. Hunter recognized it as an abandoned clothesline. Someone must have been hanging the clothes out to dry when the Insectors attacked.

Hunter grabbed the end of the line closest to him. He looped it around a nearby wooden post and pulled hard. The clothesline snapped tight at knee level.

The charging Insectors didn't see the rope in time. The front rank, six of them, tripped over the line and crashed to the ground. Their weight hitting the rope yanked Hunter off his feet. He fell to the dirt as well.

Corona turned as the second rank of bugs crashed into their fallen comrades.

"Corona! Look out!" Hunter sputtered.

Venus spun around and charged into the ambushers. Corona's lance struck two of the bugs, knocking them flat. Venus's legs whirled like a tornado, felling four more.

The three bugs left standing fled back toward their own

army, away from Corona. Venus webbed the rest of the Insectors as they tried to get up.

Corona nodded to Hunter but didn't smile. "I thought I told you to stay near the reservoir," she said.

"I saw you were in danger," he replied. "I couldn't let them ambush you."

"Well, grab yourself a 'pede weapon, then," Corona said. "And try not to get killed."

Hunter selected a metal-tipped club and took his place among the people defending the town. He tried to keep close to Corona, but Venus gave the rider much more mobility than Hunter could muster.

She and the other Spider Riders leaped among their foes, using their lances to mow down the 'pedes. Fighting the enemy from two sides had bought the Turandot time, but they were still vastly outnumbered.

Hunter dodged between attackers, trying his best to keep out of harm's way. Several times he used his captured club to ward off Centipedian blows. Every time a 'pede hit him, Hunter's arms ached. His club soon felt very, very heavy.

A 'pede stabbed at Hunter with a spear. Hunter barely managed to smash the weapon to the ground. With all his remaining strength, he swung back and knocked the Centipedian over. Venus webbed Hunter's foe before it could rise again.

Hunter started to wave a thank-you to the spider, then stopped. Venus *was* a giant spider, after all!

He noticed that Corona and the other riders looked almost as tired as he felt—and the villagers looked even worse. Scrapes traced across the riders' armor where the bugs had stabbed at them. One blow had sliced through the tattered pack on Corona's back. Inside, something glittered brightly. Hunter had neither the time nor the energy to wonder about the pack's contents.

The Insectors finished reinforcing their rickety bridge. They swarmed over it toward the village in ever greater numbers. The lead Centipedian rode onto the span, on the back of his gigantic red scorpion. An inhuman lipless smile creased the Insector commander's face.

A lucky stab from a bug lance knocked Corona off Venus. She landed hard, gasping for breath. The 'pedes swarmed in around her, looking to finish her off. The press of the crowd kept Venus from immediately reaching Corona. An Insector aimed his spear for her heart.

Hunter raced forward and clobbered the bug on the back of the head with his club. The Insector crashed, unmoving, to the ground.

Hunter bulled through the bugs and helped Corona to her feet. "Thanks," she said. Venus burst through the crowd, throwing bugs aside as she came. Frightened of the spider's wrath, the Centipedians fell back. Venus extended a foreleg, and Corona stepped up onto the arachnid's back.

"Corona," Hunter said breathlessly. "We can't win fighting like this. There are too many of them."

"Then we will die trying," Corona replied. She and Venus turned to face the enemy once more.

"I have an idea!" Hunter said. "It's something I saw in an old mov—" he began. Then, realizing the Turandot might not know about movies, he corrected himself. "It's an old battle tactic I learned about."

"Go on," Corona said.

"The bug army is all in the river valley," Hunter said. "If the river flooded, it would wash them all away."

"Do you have water powers?" Corona asked. "Because none of the rest of us do."

"We don't need special powers," Hunter said. "We just need to break the dam on top of the cliff. The water will rush down and get rid of the bugs."

A light of understanding flashed in Corona's eyes. "That might work," she said.

"Do you have any explosives?" Hunter asked.

"Any what?" she replied.

"Some force to shatter stone," Hunter explained. "The plan is no good without a way to break the dam. Do you think your energy blasts could do it?"

"Our manacles are running low on power," Corona said, "but we can try. I'll coordinate with Igneous and Magma. You get the villagers to pull back. We don't want anyone to drown."

"No one but the bugs," Hunter said.

Corona turned toward her fellow warriors. Magma and Igneous stood on the other side of the river, surrounded by Insectors—much too far away to hear anything she might say.

Hunter didn't know how she would manage, but he decided he had to trust her. He called to the villagers, urging them to move back. The townsfolk resisted, looking at him suspiciously. "Corona has a plan!" he explained.

Apparently, the village people were used to trusting the Spider Riders. Mention of Corona was all it took to convince them. They beat a quick retreat to the ground above the floodplain.

They drew back so quickly, in fact, that the Insectors seemed confused. The Centipedian commander, now in the middle of crossing the bridge, looked around. He laughed—a horrible hissing sound—and ordered his troops forward.

Magma's and Igneous's spiders leaped backward, quickly carrying their riders to the edge of the irrigated fields.

As one, the three Spider Riders turned toward the cliff face. They raised their metal bracelets. Power blasted forth from all their upraised weapons.

Spider Rider energy ripped into the dam. The support rocks at the dam's base shattered.

With a thundering roar, the dam burst.

9
A Wave of Victory

Hunter cheered, but no one heard him over the noise of the crumbling dam.

The water of the reservoir roared through the breach in the wall. Tons of liquid thundered over the cliff face. In an instant, the waterfall grew to ten times its normal size.

The Centipedians looked up, startled, as a huge tidal wave rushed down the river toward them. The bug general barked orders to his troops, but the noise of the deluge smothered his commands.

The cascading water crashed against the Insectors like a wave against an anthill. The bugs' makeshift bridge smashed into kindling. The commander and his scorpion disappeared under the swirling, debris-filled liquid.

The wave flooded the farm fields quickly. The Centipedians who had been battling there turned to run away—too late. Igneous, Magma, and Corona—on spiderback—deftly scuttled to safety before the waters reached them.

The deluge swept through the floodplain and down toward the distant lake, taking most of the Centipedian army with it. The Spider Riders quickly webbed and captured the few bugs that remained. They found no sign of the Insector commander.

"Curse him!" Magma said. "I wanted his life force medallion for my trophy wall!"

"Probably he got swept into the open water," Igneous noted. "Once our main forces arrive, I'll have patrols sweep the area. I expect we'll turn that 'pede up soon enough."

"Don't be too sure," Corona said. "He's clever, that one. He tried to use our own flanking maneuver against us. He might have succeeded, too, if not for Hunter."

"The spy?" Magma said, surprised.

"Yes," Corona said. "He warned me about the attack. He suggested causing the dam to fail, too."

"That was a clever plan, Earthen, or whoever you are," Magma said. He flashed Hunter a wry smile.

Igneous nodded. "A good plan," he said. "The fields can be replanted, but if the Centipedians had taken this village...." He looked at Corona and Magma. "Well, at the least, it would have brought the Insectors a step closer to Arachnia city." He fell silent for a moment, then said, "Come on. Reinforcements are on the way. We should dispatch any Insectors that remain."

"By 'dispatch,' does he mean *kill?*" Hunter asked Corona.

"No," she replied. "Spider Riders do not kill if they can help it. An Insector is *dispatched* when its life force medallion is removed."

"And what does that do?" Hunter asked.

"Removing the medallion turns their bodies to mist. Their essence remains captive in the medallion," she said.

"Like what you did to the mantis when we first met," Hunter said. That seemed like ages ago now.

"Yes," Corona replied. "We keep Insector life force medallions as trophies of our victories. If you were a Spider Rider, you would have earned your share of medallions today."

Hunter nodded. "If I were a Spider Rider...," he thought.

Of course, he didn't want to ride on the back of a giant spider. Ugh! Could life get any worse? All he really wanted to do was go home.

But he couldn't do that on his own. He didn't know his way around this world, for one thing. And he had no idea how to get back to the hole in the "sky." Sticking with the Spider Riders seemed his best bet for now. He would just have to put up with the creepy spiders.

Hunter knew he could tolerate the arachnids if he tried. He made the decision then and there to do whatever it took to get home.

Hunter helped clean up some of the mess from the flood while Corona, Magma, and Igneous finished webbing and dispatching the Insectors who hadn't been washed away. Only high-ranking bugs had medallions, it seemed—and there were few of those in this bunch, just subcommanders for the lead Insector, who had been swept downstream.

As Hunter worked, four more Spider Riders galloped in, led by a tall, slender young woman about Magma's age. The other riders called her Petra. Though Petra's reinforcements hadn't come in time for the battle, Hunter was glad they'd come at all.

Hunter thought he'd done quite well for himself during the fighting. Sure, he'd made mistakes and almost gotten Corona killed by accident, but he'd also helped out. He'd come up with the signal flare—though the reinforcements arrived a bit late. He'd also used the old cartoon clothesline play on the charging 'pedes. That ploy might have saved Corona's life. Plus, breaking the dam to wash away their enemies had worked perfectly.

He'd helped vanquish the Insectors! Not bad for an earth kid who hadn't even suspected Arachnia existed this morning.

"Hunter Steele," Corona called.

Hunter turned as she galloped up on Venus, fighting down his fear of the giant spider. Being apart from the spiders, even for a little while, had been a relief. Venus gazed intently at him with her six green eyes.

"Time to go," Corona said.

"Go where?" Hunter asked.

"To the city," she replied. She adjusted the tattered pack on her back. Again, Hunter caught a glimpse of something shiny inside. "Prince Lumen—the heir to the throne and our commander—will want us to report in," Corona explained.

"Couldn't you just take me home?" Hunter asked.

"That's for the prince to decide," Igneous interjected. His spider, Flame, fell in next to Venus.

Magma rode Brutus up beside them, as well. "Better hope," Magma said to Hunter, "that the prince doesn't decide you're a spy." Then he, too, spotted the glittering object in Corona's backpack.

Corona noticed his glance but made no mention of it. "If Hunter's a spy, he's a very clever one," she said. "He helped defeat a whole Centipedian army. I don't know how that could play into Mantid's plans."

"Who knows how the bug-in-chief thinks?" Magma scoffed. His spider turned as if to leave. "Well, thank you all for helping to protect this village," he said. "I guess my job is done here, so I'll be moving on to my next assignment."

"You're going?" Hunter asked.

"Of course," Magma replied. "I'm a mercenary. I go where I'm paid to go."

"I thought you were a Spider Rider," Hunter said.

"He's a free lance," Corona said, "not part of the corps."

"And happy to be that way," Magma quipped.

Corona and Igneous looked at each other for a moment. Again, Hunter got the feeling they were exchanging invisible signals of some kind.

"Magma," Igneous said, "I would like you to accompany us to Arachnia."

When Magma seemed about to refuse, Igneous added, "I'm sure the prince will make it worth your while."

Reluctantly, Magma nodded his head. He glanced from Corona's backpack to Igneous. "Well, when you put it that way...," he said.

Corona knelt down on Venus's back and offered Hunter a hand up. "Time to go," she said.

"Couldn't I just walk to the city?" Hunter asked.

All three Spider Riders laughed as Corona pulled Hunter aboard.

The trip to Arachnia took surprisingly little time. Hunter remained unsure how to measure time in this strange world where the sun never changed, but he guessed the trek took about forty-five minutes. Forests, rivers, and plains flew by as the three riders and their reluctant passenger galloped home.

Gradually, the city of Arachnia emerged from the distant haze. The capital was huge, covering the top of an immense steep-sided plateau. A fortified stone wall, at least fifty feet high, circled the city. Guards and sentries, dressed in militia armor, patrolled the top of the wall.

Though Hunter could see only a few buildings from the plain below, he guessed there were more than a thousand houses in the city. The royal castle rose above all the rest. Its twisting towers thrust proudly into the tropical sky. Colorful pennants fluttered from flagpoles attached to the keep's uppermost roofs. The banners were deep blue, blazoned with eight golden stars set in a pattern like a spider's eyes.

Hunter repressed a shudder. Spiders—ugh! Everything was spiders here! Now that he noticed it, even the castle itself looked like it was assembled of huge, stone spiders!

His gaze wandered across the tall cliffs and high city walls. "I don't see any stairs or gateways," he said to Corona. "Are they on the other side?"

"Watch," Corona said with a smile. "And hang on."

The spiders charged full-speed at the cliff. When they reached it, they raced up the sheer face without even breaking stride. Hunter gritted his teeth and hung on for dear life. He squinched his eyes shut and tried not to think of the world falling away below his feet.

A few moments later, Corona said, "It's all right now. You can open your eyes." She sounded quite amused.

Hunter opened his eyes. He and the riders stood in the middle of a wide plaza inside the city wall. Magma and Igneous chuckled and shook their heads.

"Must be his first time on spiderback," Magma said good-naturedly. "Some spy you've caught!"

"His lack of experience on spiderback proves he is not one of us," Igneous put in. "Even the youngest of our people have ridden on a spider at some time in their lives."

"Perhaps it proves that he is, indeed, Earthen," Corona suggested.

"Corona, please," Igneous said. "Keep quiet about that. We don't want people to worry."

"Yes," Magma agreed. "You know how Turandot feel about Earthen. And who can blame them? For a mercenary like me, though, more war means more work."

Hunter's face reddened. He didn't like being the center of this kind of attention. "So, you just climb straight up the wall to get into the city?" he asked. "Every time?"

"Yes," Corona replied. "We have no stairs for our enemies to climb, nor gates for them to breach. That helps keep Arachnia and her citizens safe. To enter the city, you must climb the wall and pass the sentries. We have other safeguards, as well."

"*Had* other safeguards you mean," Magma began. "That wall won't keep the bugs out much longer, if—"

Stern looks from Igneous and Corona stopped him midsentence.

"If they're of a mind to attack," Magma finished. "You know how single-minded Insectors are." He shrugged and smiled at Hunter.

"Actually, I *don't* know," Hunter said.

Magma merely shook his head.

Up close, the architecture of the castle looked even more spiderlike. Tall, arching braces reminded Hunter of huge arachnid legs. The curves of the walls looked like spidery bodies. It was as though the largest spiders ever had been turned to stone and perched on top of one another. The castle's windows looked out from the spiders' "eyes."

Corona dismounted and helped Hunter off Venus's back. The other riders stepped down, too, and all three spiders wandered off over one of the castle walls.

"Where are the spiders going?" Hunter asked, glad to see them leave.

"To relax," Corona replied. "They fought hard today and deserve a rest."

Hunter thought it odd that no one came to take the beasts. Instead, the spiders just walked away on their own. "How much freedom do the Turandot allow their mounts?" he wondered. The thought of giant spiders roaming free within the city made his stomach clench.

"This way," Igneous said. He took a position in front of Hunter; Corona placed herself behind him. They walked through the wide castle doors with Hunter between them. Magma meandered at their side, occasionally stopping to admire some detail of the architecture or a painting hanging on the wall.

Artwork lined the long, arching hallway leading to the throne room. Tapestries depicted Spider Riders battling against Insector armies. Portraits of riders adorned the walls. Statues of riders filled niches in the stonework. Hunter was struck again by the fact that none of the riders looked very old.

Two tall golden doors filled the portal at the end of the hall. Sculptures of spiders, their many legs intertwined, covered the doors. Hunter noticed that the doors seemed sealed together—the legs of the sculptures all locked into one another.

As they approached, the golden spider legs untwined, and the doors swung easily inward of their own volition. Hunter glanced nervously at the doors. Were those *real* golden spiders? He tried not to think about it.

The throne room on the other side of the doors was even more lavish than the palace hall. Brightly colored mosaics featuring spiders, naturally, covered the floor. Lace curtains woven in a web pattern draped the windows. Huge portraits of kings and queens—grown-ups, unlike the riders—hung on the walls. An empty golden throne sat on a dais at the far side of the room.

Closer to the entrance a number of chairs were grouped near a fireplace. As the riders entered the room, three people got up from the chairs. One was an older man with graying hair. A crown with six blue gems rested on his forehead. Deep blue robes with golden spider designs covered his slender body. His eyes sparkled with quick intelligence.

A boy about Hunter's age—or perhaps a year or two younger—stood next to the king. His dark hair almost covered his serious eyes. Carefully cut silken clothing, with a small cape at the shoulders, adorned his slender form. On one wrist, he wore the manacle bracelet of a Spider Rider. A short sword dangled from a scabbard strapped to his waist. Hunter assumed this was the prince.

A younger girl bounced out of her chair and stood beside the older man. She tried to look grown-up and solemn, but her darting, curious eyes betrayed her. She was dressed casually—too casually for her surroundings—but her clothes were well made. Her braided hair was secured with a silver spider brooch. She smiled at Hunter.

"Lumen has informed us that your mission was a success," the older man said to Corona and Igneous. "We are pleased."

Corona and Igneous bowed. Magma dipped his knees slightly.

"Thank you, King Arachna," Igneous said. "We are honored to serve you and the kingdom."

The king nodded at Igneous. "You know the importance of your work to our kingdom," he said. "These are dark times. But I trust that the leadership of my son will bring us back to the light." He turned to the prince, looking slightly worried. "Guide your riders well, my son. I go to attend to our people."

Prince Lumen bowed to the king. "I will do my best, Father," he said.

"Me, too!" piped the girl.

The king smiled at her. "Come, Sparkle," he said. "Councils of war are not for one who has not yet won her manacle."

"But I'm a Spider Rider!" the girl protested.

"You ride a spider," Lumen said, "but you are not yet one of us."

"It's no fair!" the girl said. "Why does my brother get to lead and I don't?"

"Come, dear," her father said to the young princess. "I will explain it all to you...again." He cast a longing glance toward Prince Lumen, then escorted the girl out of the room.

Lumen breathed a sigh of relief as they left. Then he drew himself up regally.

"Is this the supposed Earthen that Ebony told me about?" Lumen asked Igneous.

"Yes," Igneous replied. "But he could be an Insector spy."

"He did save us, my prince," Corona said. "It was his idea that allowed us to defeat the Centipedian army."

Prince Lumen nodded. "Yes," he said. "But that does not completely prove his loyalty. Ebony and I must think on this. Escort him to a waiting room while we consider." He snapped his fingers, and a side door opened. Two adult guards entered and came to Hunter's side.

"Waiting room?" Hunter said. After all he'd been through today, he didn't feel pleased about this. "Look—" he began.

The prince silenced him with a gesture. "Do not make me act in haste," Lumen said, "or I will judge you harshly."

The guards escorted Hunter out of the throne room and into a small chamber nearby. They closed the doors behind him and clicked the lock into place.

Hunter tried the door handle, just to make sure. Yep. Locked in. He sat down on the floor and put his head in his hands. At this rate, he would *never* get home!

10
The Breakout

Hunter looked around the windowless room. It was probably very nice by Turandot standards, but it had far too many spidery things for his taste. The vaulted ceiling looked like a spider spreading its legs down over him. Eight-legged designs covered the draperies on the wall. Spiders modeled in silver crawled up the candleholders. Spider motifs decorated the frame of the king's portrait hanging on one wall. Iron spiders held the logs in the fireplace.

Only the wooden bookcase across from the portrait seemed completely spider-free. Although, now that Hunter looked closer, many of the books did feature spider illustrations on their spines.

The creepiness of the whole day was taking its toll on him. He felt exhausted. He blew out all the candles in the room but one, then went to a padded couch that didn't look *too* spiderlike and lay down.

Hunter closed his eyes and tried not to think about being surrounded by so many spiders. But even with his eyes shut, he couldn't sleep. He still saw spiders everywhere, crawling inside his mind. He heard them, too, creaking and scraping and...

Wait a minute. That was a *real* sound he'd heard. Not his imagination. It wasn't a spider, either. It sounded like a door slowly opening.

Had they come to get him already?

Cautiously, Hunter cracked open one eye and looked toward the door. It remained closed tight, but someone was in the room, sneaking around.

Not wanting to betray himself to the intruder, Hunter looked around, as much as he could without moving his head. A small figure stood in the shadows nearby, staring at him.

He felt relieved that the figure was human. Then anger rose within him. Was this how they would treat him, like a pet in a zoo? Would the Turandot all come in turn to gaze at him while he slept?

Hunter's determination to get back home became stronger than ever. He was just about to leap from the couch when the small figure gasped and backed away. It was Princess Sparkle. She must have figured out that Hunter wasn't asleep, because she quickly moved to the carved fireplace mantel.

Before Hunter realized what was happening, her fingers played across the surface of a few spidery sculptures. A panel in the wall next to the fireplace opened, and she slipped through.

Hunter sprang from the couch and dived through the opening before it snapped shut.

He got to his feet, stood perfectly still, and listened. As he did, he heard light footsteps scampering away.

A light flared in the distance, and Sparkle peered back toward him. "Is anyone there?" she whispered fearfully.

Hunter kept quiet. It seemed obvious now that the princess's visit to spy on him hadn't been ordered by her brother or her father.

"I know you followed me," Sparkle said. Her voice sounded uncertain, like someone whistling past a graveyard to build up her courage. "You'd better go back, or you'll be in even worse trouble."

Hunter remained silent. The passage between them was narrow and, much to Hunter's disgust, filled with spiderwebs. But he was still out of reach of her light.

"Y-you have to be part of the royal family to use this passage," the princess continued. "It's *forbidden*. If anybody finds you..."

The princess's threat rang hollow. "She's not supposed to be here, either," Hunter thought.

"Don't say I didn't warn you," she said. With that, Sparkle blew out her candle and dashed away from him, into the darkness. A moment later, a door at the far end of the passage slid open. Hunter saw Sparkle silhouetted against the opening for a moment. Then she darted through and out of sight.

Hunter wished he'd grabbed a candle before diving through the secret door. How was he going to find the door at the other end and open it without being able to see anything?

Well, at least he wasn't trapped inside the "waiting room" any longer.

He moved cautiously forward, trying not to bump into anything, searching for the exit. As he drew near to the spot where he'd last seen Sparkle, he heard voices.

Hunter froze and listened.

"...Very lucky on today's venture," he heard Prince Lumen say.

Hunter smiled. This passageway not only ran to the waiting room, it also ran behind the throne room. Perhaps

Sparkle had even been eavesdropping on her brother before coming to spy on him!

"The 'pede commander you faced is known as Centok," the prince said. "He's very ambitious. Centok is trying to gain the favor of Mantid—perhaps to become one of the Big Four Insectors himself."

"Today's defeat probably won't help him in that respect," Magma noted. It sounded to Hunter as though the mercenary rider was smiling.

"Don't underestimate him," the prince said curtly.

"Prince Lumen is right," Corona said. "Even in this battle, Centok tried to turn our own tactics against us."

"That makes him smarter than most Insectors," Igneous said, "but their main strategy is still brute force. Our training gives us the advantage, as does our mind-talk ability."

"Mind talk?" Hunter thought. "I wonder what that means?"

"Neither training nor telepathy will protect us if Mantid's forces attack us now," Lumen said, his voice grave. He took a deep breath. "Igneous, are you sure this mercenary can be trusted?"

"Pay my price and you can trust me until the hatchlings come home," Magma put in.

"We have to trust him, Your Highness," Igneous replied. "During the battle, he saw Corona's ... burden. We have no choice but to pay him."

"He glimpsed the *shard?*" Lumen asked.

"The pack holding it became ripped during the battle," Corona said. "The Earthen boy saw it as well, I think, but he would not know what it was."

"Whereas, I knew immediately," Magma added. "I have grasped something that our Insector enemies have not—that without the Oracle, Arachnia is almost defenseless."

None of this made much sense to Hunter. What shard? What oracle? What had he seen that he wasn't supposed to see? And what was that business about telepathy?

"Mantid must suspect," Igneous said, "or he would never have stolen the shards of the Oracle in the first place."

"Mantid is cautious, though," Lumen said. "He waits to strike until victory can be certain. As ruler of the Insectors, he can do nothing less. That is why he lets others, such as his Big Four Insectors or Centok, fight his battles for him."

"And that is why, with or without the Oracle, we may still defeat him," Igneous concluded.

"*May*," Prince Lumen agreed. "But I need to be *certain*. You three must find the remaining pieces of the Oracle. Magma, I am hiring you to help with the job."

"It will be my pleasure, Prince," Magma replied graciously.

The prince sounded stiff and formal, as though Magma's politeness caught him off guard. "We must act quickly, before our enemies discover our weakness," he said. "My father has entrusted this job to me, and we must not fail. Every day without the Oracle brings Arachnia closer to disaster."

"It's funny," Magma mused, "that an Earthen should appear during this time of crisis. Isn't that what the prophecy foretells?"

"Yes," Corona said. "Though I know that you, Magma, do not believe in the prophecy any more than Igneous does."

"I believe in the prophecy," Igneous countered. "I just don't believe that *this* boy is the one foretold. Look at him! He knows nothing of our world. Our spiders seem to frighten him. As I said earlier, it's far more likely that he's a spy sent by Mantid to vex us in this time of crisis."

"I'm not sure...," Lumen said.

"Or perhaps this crisis *proves* he is the one foretold," Corona suggested.

"In either case, I do not like it," Lumen said. "Don't we have enough troubles already? I would consult the Oracle if she were not lost to us."

Hunter felt puzzled again. So this Oracle was a person? But if she was, what did these "shards" have to do with it? Perhaps if he listened more closely, he could figure it out.

He pressed his ear to the wall nearest the voices.

As he did, his hand came to rest on something cold and spiderlike.

Hunter yelped and stumbled back, tripping over his own feet.

"What was that?" Igneous's voice boomed.

Hunter groped around in the darkness, trying to get his bearings. He put his hand against a wall and stood.

Suddenly, the wall gave way and Hunter tumbled out, into the throne room.

The Spider Riders quickly surrounded him.

11
The Spy

Dungobeet scampered into the grand audience chamber of Mantid the Magnificent. The chamber was a huge, sparsely furnished room in Mantid's fortress. The vaulted walls of the room reached high overhead. They arced toward a metal thronelike chair flanked by two waist-high marble tables at the far end of the chamber. The design of the room focused all attention on the chair's occupant, Mantid, the ruler of the Insectors. The chamber's architecture made Mantid look even more powerful and impressive than usual.

Dungobeet didn't need to be impressed; he feared and worshiped Mantid already. Three fist-size message bugs buzzed around the humanoid beetle, following his every move. Dungobeet wasn't very tall or imposing as far as Insectors went. He had the usual carapace armor and frightening-looking claws and barbs on his exoskeleton, but he didn't like using them. He preferred to let others fight his battles.

His message bugs buzzed into every corner of the Insector kingdoms, reporting everything they saw to him. Dungobeet in turn, reported to Mantid.

At the far end of the room, Mantid turned his chair to face his underling. Dungobeet snatched up the circling bugs and stuffed them into a pouch he carried on his back. The beetleoid knew that the head Insector despised unnecessary distractions.

Dungobeet dropped to the floor and knelt in front of his master. "Great Mantid the Malevolent," he began, "I have news."

Magnificent robes and armor covered nearly every inch of the bug ruler's body. He was both great mystery and fearful warrior supreme. Dungobeet would have swallowed his tongue—if he'd had one—as Mantid turned his cold, calculating gaze on the smaller Insector.

"Of course you have news," Mantid hissed. "Or I would not tolerate your presence. Speak!"

"Centok's raiding army has been defeated," Dungobeet reported. "The river rose up against them and washed them away—we're not sure how. Centok himself escaped and awaits your next orders."

The scythelike limbs projecting from Mantid's armor twitched angrily. Dungobeet backed away a few steps. "Th-there's more, master," he said.

Mantid's icy voice echoed throughout the great room. "Continue."

"M-more bad news, I'm afraid," Dungobeet said. "The Spider Riders also captured one of your mantis minions. They have regained one of the shards."

One of Mantid's serrated claws flashed out and crashed into the marble table on his right. The table broke in half and crumbled into pieces.

Dungobeet jumped back and lowered his head to the floor, cowering. "It's not m-my fault, m-master!" he said.

"No," Mantid snapped. "Never your fault."

Dungobeet got the feeling that Mantid didn't really mean that. The smaller Insector quaked within his shell. He waited—either for death or for the master's next orders.

"Send out your spies," Mantid said. "Contact those guarding the remaining shards of the Oracle. Make sure their defenses are strong. The Spider Riders will be coming."

"Y-yes, master."

"And when the riders come," Mantid growled, "tell our allies to kill them."

"Um...hi," Hunter said. He pushed himself up off the throne room floor, into a half-kneeling position. He forced a smile.

"What is *he* doing here!" Prince Lumen said, so surprised that his young voice almost cracked.

Igneous stepped away from the spider-shaped carving he'd used to open the secret panel. "Skulking in the royal passageway," he said. "I can't say I'm surprised, but I am disappointed."

"I was just...exploring," Hunter insisted.

"What did you hear?" Lumen asked, his face red with anger.

"Look, I'm sorry," Hunter said. "I didn't mean to intrude, but I've had kind of a bad day. I've fallen to the center of the earth, I've been attacked by giant bugs, I've been tied up, sleep-darted, carried all across this blazingly hot world...." His embarrassment was fast giving way to anger. "I help to save a village, and then, for my trouble, I get locked into a tiny room filled with spidery furniture." He got up and dusted the cobwebs off his clothes. "And all I really want to do is go home. Can I go home now...please?"

The prince and the other Spider Riders stood stunned by his outburst.

"He did help save the village," Corona finally said. "And he protected my back from a Centipedian attack. Igneous may think Hunter Steele is a spy, but I do not." She looked at the prince, as if trying to sway his opinion.

Prince Lumen seemed torn. He paced the room while Corona and Igneous took up places next to Hunter, awaiting the prince's decision.

"Where is this home of yours?" Lumen asked Hunter.

"On the surface of the world," he said. "You know ... topside. At the end of that long tunnel I slid down to get here."

Igneous rolled his eyes. "The Earthen thing again!" he said. "Do you know how long it's been since a *real* Earthen came to Arachnia?"

"It's the truth," Hunter insisted. "Look at my clothes. Does anyone down here dress like this?"

Lumen took a deep breath and sighed it out. "The manner of your dress is strange," he said, "but the appearance of a *true* Earthen bodes ill for Arachnia. We all know the prophecies." He gazed levely at Hunter.

Hunter read determination and just a bit of fear behind the prince's eyes.

"Ebony and I agree, it would be best to return you home," Lumen said. "However, that is not within my power."

Hunter's heart fell. He'd thought for a moment that he'd found a way out of this awful spidery place. But if the prince couldn't help him ...

"All things fall to the center," Lumen continued. "Our ancestors fell into this world, much as you have. Only one of them—the Arachna-Master—ever returned home."

Hunter brightened. "Somebody got back to the surface?"

"It's merely a legend," Igneous said.

Corona explained. "Arachna-Master Iridium, one of the

greatest of our order, is said to have braved the hazards and climbed to the surface. That was so long ago, though, that it's impossible to tell whether the story is truth or myth."

"I favor myth," Igneous said.

"Me, too," Magma put in. "Besides, why would anyone want to climb to a world where there are no Spider Riders?"

Hunter kept silent but thought, "I was very happy living without giant spiders. The regular kind were bad enough!" His mind raced furiously, trying to figure out some way to get home.

"Since return of the Earthen to his home is impossible," the prince said, "and since he has no other training, he should join our Arachnian workforce. Perhaps laboring on a farm would suit him."

"I have plenty of training," Hunter blurted. "Just because I wasn't born here doesn't mean I'm helpless! I did really well in the battle at the river!"

"That's true," Corona said. "His assistance was invaluable to our victory."

Prince Lumen rubbed his chin thoughtfully. "Perhaps, then, there is some boon we could grant him."

"Look," Hunter said, "I don't want a boon or a baboon or whatever it is you're going to grant me. If being a Spider Rider, an Arachna-Master, is what it takes to get me home, then do it. Make me a Spider Rider. Then I can find my own way home!"

Hunter could hardly believe what he'd just said, but there was no backing out now. If this was his ticket home, he'd have to take it. He'd stick with the plan no matter what.

For a moment, shocked silence filled the throne room.

"Spider Riders are sworn to defend Arachnia," Igneous said finally.

"Didn't I do that already?" Hunter asked.

"But we are sworn to protect the kingdom until *all* Insector threats are defeated," Corona put in.

"So, I'll defend your kingdom," Hunter said. "And after we've won this war, I'll try to find a way home. That seems fair."

Magma scoffed. "The war with the Insectors will *never* end!"

"Well, that's no problem, then," Hunter said, still feeling pretty angry. "Because you say that going home is impossible anyway. So, what's it going to hurt? Make me a Spider Rider."

He stood proudly, waiting for the prince's judgment. Igneous eyed him warily. Corona looked impressed by his bravery. Magma laughed.

"The kid has guts!" the mercenary said. "He almost reminds me of me!"

"And that's a good thing?" Corona asked.

"I say, let him try," Magma concluded.

All of them looked to the prince.

Lumen looked torn, as though he were having a conversation with himself. "Very well," he said finally. "Ebony has convinced me. Hunter Steele may attempt to join the ranks of the Spider Riders."

"He must take all the same tests," Igneous interjected, "endure all the same training."

"Of course," Lumen continued. "If he fails, he will join our labor force, to work in the fields for the rest of his life."

Hunter took a deep breath and gathered his courage. No matter what it took, he *would* get home!

"Okay," he said. "When do I start?"

PART TWO

SPIDER RIDERS

12
Spider Canyon

Hunter regretted his hasty request almost immediately. Becoming a Spider Rider had seemed the only way out of this crazy world at the time, but he hadn't really considered the ramifications.

Sure, becoming a rider sounded easy within the confines of a cozy throne room with no spiders around. Now, though, riding behind Corona on Venus's back once more, the situation seemed very different.

What *had* he been thinking?

Then he remembered. "Home," he thought. "I'm doing this to get home. And this is my only chance to get there."

He glanced from Corona to Igneous, riding beside them, then back again. Neither Spider Rider betrayed the slightest emotion.

The five of them—counting the spiders—had been on the move for hours now, as best Hunter could judge time in a world of eternal sunshine.

They'd shambled through jungles, up wooded hillsides, and into terrain that reminded Hunter of the badlands in old movie Westerns—lots of rocks and crevasses. Through it all, he had no idea where they were going.

He hadn't gotten much sleep in his new quarters—a sparsely furnished hole in the side of a cliff with a curtain covering the entryway to block out the ever-present light. It seemed as though his head had barely hit the pillow when Igneous and Corona dragged him out of bed to go on this trek.

No one had talked to him much since Lumen decreed Hunter could try to become a Spider Rider. Apparently, that was part of the deal. The other riders wanted to see if you could handle yourself on your own. Corona had given him only the bare essentials: "We're taking you on your first trial," she had said.

Hunter wished they would hurry up and get there already.

"Are you *sure* you can't tell me where we're going?" Hunter asked.

Neither Corona nor Igneous replied.

Ahead, the badlands gradually fell away, replaced by scrub-covered rocky hills. Between them and the hills stretched a huge, gaping chasm. It was at least a mile across and so deep that, as they rode up, Hunter couldn't see the bottom.

"Almost there," Corona said, breaking her long silence.

"Good," Hunter replied. At least, he hoped it was good. It would be good to get off spiderback, at any rate. Though they'd set up a more comfortable harness for him to ride with, the ride was still pretty bumpy.

Igneous and Corona halted their spiders near the edge of the huge pit. Igneous looked gravely at Hunter. "Ready?" he asked.

"Sure," Hunter said, not feeling very ready at all.

The spiders surged forward and over the canyon rim, climbing straight down the wall.

Hunter's heart shot up into his throat. Simultaneously, an icy chill stabbed down his spine. He still wasn't used to climbing up and down sheer walls on spiderback. But to make matters worse, the entire canyon appeared to be filled with spiderwebs!

"Wh-where are we?" Hunter asked.

"Spider Canyon," Corona replied. "Your first test as a new rider is to find your own spider."

"M-my own s-spider?" Hunter said.

"Yes," Corona replied. "There are many ways a rider finds a spider. You may be chosen, you may inherit, you may dominate, or take a trusted partner."

"What?" Hunter asked, his head still swimming. He had to get his own spider! He thought they'd start out with some kind of training first, give him a chance to get more used to the giant arachnids. This trip was rapidly turning into a nightmare—again.

"Every rider pairing is different," Corona continued. "You must find the spider that's right for you."

Hunter took a deep breath. "Okay," he said. "I think I can do that." Actually, he didn't think anything of the kind. Fear had nearly turned his insides to jelly.

The riders and Hunter reached the bottom of the canyon. Lush forest covered the canyon floor. White mist filtered through the timbers, giving the whole place a feeling of unreality. Many layers of spiderwebs, some old, some new, hung from the boughs of the trees. The sound of running water echoed to the riders from somewhere in the mist.

"So, are there many spiders here?" Hunter asked, his voice squeaking slightly.

Igneous laughed. "Why do you think it's called Spider Canyon? There are more spiders here than anyplace in Arachnia."

Hunter suppressed a shudder. He would have run, but

with the sheer canyon walls blocking his way, he had nowhere to escape to.

"A rider can find his spider anywhere," Corona explained. "But since you are new to our world"—and here she looked at Igneous, who still seemed not to believe Hunter's story—"we thought this the best place to start."

"Are there *man-eating* spiders here?" Hunter asked.

"Any spider might eat an enemy if threatened," Igneous replied. "So, be careful what you do and whom you offend." The big Turandot seemed to find the whole situation amusing.

Hunter didn't think it was funny at all.

Igneous threw him a long spiderweb rope. "Here," he said. "You'll need this." He handed Hunter a small hunting knife and a hard-shell canteen, as well. "Use these to help you survive until you find your mount."

"Aren't you staying with me?" Hunter asked, fighting the growing desperation he felt inside.

"This test is for you alone," Corona said.

"Good-bye, Earthen," Igneous said. He turned Flame around and climbed back up the canyon wall. Corona helped Hunter down off Venus's back. She and Venus turned to go, as well.

"Corona, wait!" Hunter said.

She paused.

"How am I supposed to do this?" he asked desperately.

"I told you, each rider must—"

"I know," he interjected, "'must find the spider that's right for him.' But how do I do that? How do I know that the next spider I meet won't eat me?"

"Igneous was exaggerating," Corona said. "A spider will

SPIDER RIDERS

Hunter in Pedestrian Mode

SPIDER RIDERS

Igneous in Pedestrian Mode

SPIDER RIDERS

Flame in Battle Mode

SPIDER RIDERS

Brutus in Battle Mode

SPIDER RIDERS

Magma in Pedestrian Mode

SPIDER RIDERS

Corona in Pedestrian Mode

SPIDER RIDERS

A Centipedian

SPIDER RIDERS

A Cockroach Warrior

not eat a human except in the most dire circumstances. All you need to do is talk to them, and—"

"Talk to them?" Hunter said. "What are you talking about? I've hardly heard you and the other riders say two words to your mounts."

"You are wrong, Hunter Steele," Corona said. "Venus and I speak all the time."

Hunter looked puzzled.

"We communicate through mind talk," she said. "Surely you know that."

"What's mind talk?" Hunter asked. "Is that the telepathy I heard the prince mention in the throne room?"

"Exactly."

"Well, I don't know how to do that!"

Corona paused, as if listening to something Hunter couldn't hear. "Venus says," she explained, "that you'd better learn pretty quickly if you want to survive your first test."

Hunter's heart sank. He plopped down on a rock on the canyon floor and looked disconsolate.

Corona climbed off Venus's back and put her hand on his shoulder. "Hunter, you can do it," she said. "I've seen your bravery. You have what it takes to be a Spider Rider."

Her words comforted him. He stood and dusted off his clothes. "So, how do I do this mind talk?" he asked. "Do I just think really loud at the spider? Can Venus 'hear' me thinking now?"

"No," Corona said. "After you have bonded with your spider, you may be able to speak to other spiders, if they let you. Telepathy is the spider's natural form of communication. With humans, it comes harder."

Hunter suddenly realized something. "That's how you

coordinated your attacks at the river village!" he said. "That's how you all knew when to use your energy blasts."

"Yes," Corona said. "I talk with Venus, and she communicates with the other spiders, so we all act together. Mind talk gives us an edge that the Insectors cannot match. Without it and...other advantages...the Turandot would have fallen long ago. We Spider Riders are the keystone to protecting our civilization."

"But why are you all so young?" Hunter asked. "I've never seen a grown-up rider. Are all the older riders...dead?"

Corona laughed. "The gift of mind talk fades with time," she explained. "Only those on the verge of adulthood can share the special bond with the spiders. When one gets too old, one retires to one's second profession. The first job of all capable Turandot is to be a Spider Rider."

She put her hand on his shoulder again. "Good luck, Hunter Steele," she said. "If the Oracle smiles upon you, soon you will join our ranks." She stepped away from him. "I've already stayed too long. Good-bye." She mounted Venus, and the two of them crawled up the sheer cliff face and out of the canyon.

"Choose your spider well!" she called back to him.

Hunter watched her go for a moment. Then the gravity of his situation sank in. He was stranded in a deep canyon with who-knows-how-many hostile giant spiders. He had only a rope, a canteen, and a small knife to keep himself alive.

How was he supposed to catch his own giant spider?

Just when he thought he'd hit the bottom in this crazy world, things got worse!

13
Hunting Spiders

A rustling sound interrupted Hunter feeling sorry for himself. A huge shape moved through the trees. A spider!

Hunter took a deep breath, trying to summon the courage to face the giant arachnid. He failed.

As the leaves parted and a red-and-purple spider ambled into the clearing, Hunter dove for a nearby group of rocks. He hit the ground and rolled to cover behind the big boulders. His heart pounded, and sweat poured down his skin. He felt glad that Corona couldn't see him hiding here, terrified.

Why did he ever ask to become a Spider Rider!

He heard the creature's armored legs scraping through the foliage nearby.

"You can do this!" he told himself. "You *have* to do this!" But another part of him didn't think he could do it at all. Most of Hunter believed he would die here in Spider Canyon. Either he'd be eaten by a spider, or he'd slowly starve to death, or...

He wondered if Corona and the others would come back to look for him when he didn't return. He squeezed his eyes shut and tried not to think about it. He tried not to think about the giant, unknown spider lurking so nearby.

For long minutes, his heart pounded in his ears. When the drumbeat of his blood finally stopped, he opened his eyes.

Silence filled the clearing. He peered around the rocks. The spider had gone.

Hunter cursed himself for being such a chicken. He hadn't even dared to *look* at the spider. Some hero he was turning out to be! At this rate, he would never get home.

"I will take this one step at a time," he said aloud to himself. "I will *not* give up."

As he sat there, behind the rocks, drenched with his own sweat, he came up with a plan. First, he would scout the area—that's what warriors always did in stories. He would avoid contact with the "enemy" until he knew the lay of the land.

Then he would watch the spiders and carefully select one that seemed suitable to be his mount. He knew that spiders came in many shapes and sizes. Corona's Venus was different from Igneous's Flame, who was different from Magma's Brutus.

If Hunter was going to do this, he might as well get the biggest, strongest spider he saw. Why not? There was no sense trying for second best. Choosing a small, "easy" spider would just make it harder for him to win his way back home later.

Getting home, that was what mattered. He knew he could do it if he just worked hard enough.

Having a plan made Hunter feel better, even though he hadn't actually done anything yet.

He rose from behind the rocks and paced around the clearing, getting a clear view of the trails leading out of it. The tracks in the ground indicated the trails were used by wild game insects—like giant ants and the aphids he'd seen pulling village carts—and not by the spiders themselves. With the ability to climb the trees or the canyon walls, the spiders had little need for such paths.

Walking down the trails might mark him as prey to any spiders lurking nearby. Besides, the spiderwebs seemed to grow thicker inside the jungle. And was that the scuttling of hundreds of arachnid feet he heard in the distance? Just the thought of it sent a shiver down his spine. Hunter decided not to take the trails, not unless it was absolutely necessary.

He decided, instead, to follow the cliff face. The going would be slower there, as he clambered over the rocks, but it seemed safer, as well as being more familiar to him than the jungle. There were no jungles where Hunter had grown up, but he'd climbed over a lot of rocks.

Hunter knew that on the surface some spiders liked rocky lairs, as well. He would have to be careful and keep his eye out for "trapdoors" and other spider tricks. Still, despite their enormous size, the Arachnian spiders didn't seem much different from surface spiders. At home, he could deal with spiders if he put his mind to it. There was no reason he couldn't do the same here, even if the spiders were a lot bigger.

He advanced cautiously along the cliff, keeping well away from caves or other places where giant spiders might hide. As he went he saw two black-bodied arachnids climbing down the cliff into the valley.

His heart beat rapidly as he watched them descend. Some part of him said, "Go! Catch one!" But a larger, more sensible part urged, "Wait. There are two of them. You can't tackle two. That's not the plan. Stick to the plan and you'll be fine."

But how would he tackle even *one* of the huge arachnids?

How was he supposed to catch a spider, anyway? He didn't have any nets to drop on one or a shovel to dig a pit trap. Watching the enormous beasts, Hunter began to feel more and more that this test wasn't fair.

"The prince wants me to fail," he thought. "He's sent me into this canyon just to get rid of me."

Would Corona be part of such a scheme? Hunter didn't think so. She seemed to genuinely like him. And she was the only one who really believed his story about coming from the surface world. Maybe Igneous would dump Hunter into a spider-filled pit to die, but not Corona.

"So, there *must* be a way for me to catch a spider," Hunter thought. "If Corona and Igneous did it, I can do it, too."

He watched from concealment as the two big spiders crawled past him and headed for a game trail. The two arachnids looked as alike as parent and child. One was slightly larger, and his carapace was somewhat grayer. The other was black as midnight, with powerful legs and jaws. He followed where the other spider led.

"If I see a spider like that alone, I'll catch it," Hunter resolved.

Just before the spiders disappeared into the trees, the larger one turned back. Its six red eyes peered toward Hunter, as though sensing he was there.

Hunter ducked back out of sight, a cold sweat breaking over his body. A memory of falling into the huge web on his way to the center of the earth flashed through his mind. The eyes of this spider looked very much like those eyes. Could they be one and the same?

Hunter gathered his courage and peered around the rock

to get a better look. But by then both spiders had vanished into the foliage.

Hunter returned to scouting the land. As he climbed over the rocks at the edge of the cliff, he looked for ways out of the canyon. "Leaving is still an option," a small part of his mind said. The larger part, though, knew that if he left now he would probably never get back home. "Stick to the goal," he told himself. "You can do it." The more cautious part of him still looked for an exit, just in case.

He felt almost relieved when he didn't find any easy way out. Though the spiders had no trouble scaling the sheer walls, the cliffs were well beyond Hunter's rock climbing experience.

"I guess I have to be a hero whether I want to or not," he thought. "So I might as well stop worrying and get to it."

Time had no meaning in the Inner World, where the sun never set. Hunter took to gauging the days by how hungry he felt and how tired he got. Finding food wasn't too difficult. There were plenty of fruit trees to support wild herbivore insects—or a hungry human—in the canyon bottom.

Several times he followed some giant ants to an orchard of ripe fruit. The big insects didn't frighten him the way the spiders did. Once, a swarm of spiders attacked the grazing ants. Hunter left quickly and counted himself lucky to get away. He stopped following game insects after that.

Water proved trickier to find than food. Hunter often heard the sounds of running water within the jungle, but he didn't want to get lost by venturing too far from the edge. The canyon was miles wide and many miles long. It contained plenty of places for him to vanish forever, especially with wild spiders scampering about.

So, Hunter kept to the sides near the walls, which limited his water to the occasional trickles that ran down the cliff face.

Hunter saw many spiders as he traveled—yellow swift ones, green jumpers, red web-spinners, wolflike predators. None were as large or powerful as the two black spiders he'd encountered earlier. Now that he'd worked up his courage, he refused to take anything less than the best mount he could find. After a while, the spiders seemed less scary, even though there were an awful lot of them crawling about.

He didn't sleep well in the canyon. The ever-blazing sun kept him awake, even though he was exhausted much of the time. He couldn't bear to sleep in a cliff-side nook, in case it was the secret lair of some spider. Sheltering under the trees didn't appeal for the same reason. When he finally confronted one of the eight-legged brutes, he wanted to do it on his terms.

So when he got tired, he cut some large, oval-shaped leaves with his knife and constructed a makeshift tent, well off the game trails.

After his third sleep, he saw the black spiders again, traveling together, the larger one always slightly ahead of the other. They looked magnificent, in a spidery way. Hunter reminded himself that if he ever saw one of them alone, he would catch it.

After spying on various spiders for nearly a week, Hunter's heart stopped pounding every time he saw one. He still hadn't found the right spider to approach, though.

And despite his growing courage, he hadn't really come up

with a plan for how to catch one, either. Corona's suggestion that he mind-talk to the spiders seemed completely absurd.

Several times, from behind cover, he attempted to send a spider a telepathic message. "Come here!" and "Roll over!" didn't work. Nor did "Heel!" or "Fetch!"

Hunter threw a stick while trying this last command. The bright red leaper spotted the flying branch and turned, not toward the stick but toward Hunter. He ducked back behind a rock and waited until the spider left. No sense trying to catch a mad spider with just his bare hands.

Corona had been right about one thing at least: the spiders, thankfully, didn't seem to hunt humans.

After his next sleep, Hunter watched some blue-backed, spindle-legged arachnids playing in the treetops. They looked harmless enough, and he hardly felt any fear at all, but they weren't the kind of spider he wanted.

Just after waking that morning, he'd finally come up with a plan to catch his mount. He based the idea on the old rope around the leg trick, a ploy favored by cowboys, as well as hunters in old cartoons.

The plan was simple: he would make his rope into a noose—something he'd figured out how to do over the previous few days—and place the noose in a spider's path. When the spider came by, Hunter would snare one of its legs and wrap the other end of the rope around a tree.

The spider would buck like a bronco, then tire. When it did, Hunter would jump on its back and "break" it—the way cowboys broke horses.

He felt pleased with himself for coming up with this plan. It seemed, to him, to have a good chance of working. Once he finally captured his spider, he would also be able to get out of the canyon. After a week or so among the cliffs and trees and webs, Hunter was longing for his tiny room in Arachnia city.

After lunch, Hunter spotted one of the big, black spiders traveling alone. It was the larger of the two, the one with the slightly gray carapace and the red eyes.

Hunter noticed now that this spider moved somewhat more slowly than the others in the valley. Perhaps it was older, but Hunter deemed that a good thing. He could catch an old spider to train with, then trade up to a better one later, when he had some experience.

Hunter cautiously trailed the spider through the edge of the forest, making sure not to be seen. When the big arachnid stopped to drink at a tiny pool, Hunter moved ahead of it. The black spider seemed to be hunting along one of the forest's many trails.

As silently as he could, Hunter cut ahead on the trail and laid his noose. Then he hid in the foliage beside a wide tree and waited.

Soon, the big black spider ambled past his hiding place. Hunter yanked on the noose. It cinched tight around the spider's leg.

The spider reared.

Hunter looped his rope around the big tree to secure it.

The spider took off running. The rope yanked tight, pulling Hunter off his feet before he could tie down the line.

He fumbled desperately at the cord, trying to make it hold. All he succeeded in doing, though, was looping the rope tightly around his own wrist.

Hunter smashed into the tree as the spider kept going. The cord yanked him around the trunk and dragged him across the ground.

The big, black arachnid galloped away, pulling Hunter behind it.

14
Specters of Doom

The grand meeting chamber of Mantid the Malevolent was as glorious as his audience chamber. Polished translucent quartz made up the walls. By pressing one's face to a wall, one could see out to the vast Insector lands beyond. From a distance, though, the walls appeared nearly opaque—only pale shadows from outside penetrated their surface.

The quartz walls allowed Mantid to see out as he pleased, while focusing the attention of any guests in the room on the Insector ruler himself.

Mantid sat on a platform near the side of the room opposite the entryway. The walls arched overhead, supported by great vaulting ribs. The whole looked something like the interior skeleton of a huge insect. The motif suited Mantid just fine.

The platform he sat on rose up from the floor on six sturdy legs, all arced to match the shape of the room. The result was that the master looked as though he were sitting astride the back of a gigantic, translucent bug. His seat grew out of the platform, as though it were a saddle attached to the insect's back.

Those who met with the Insector chief did not get such grand seats. Their chairs rested on the room's main floor. The lower seats looked as though they were composed of the skeletons of dead bugs—which, indeed, they were. Some of these chairs were large, others small. The ones being used today were the largest, other than the one occupied by Mantid himself. Mantid's current guests were the most important Insectors in the realm—the Big Four, as they were known.

One was a gigantic beetle warrior, Stags. His armor glistened even in the chamber's diffuse light. On his right sat Grasshop, a slender, armored villain. Grasshop fidgeted nervously with a small, rodlike device he'd brought with him. He was the inventor of the group. The invention sparked slightly as he toyed with it. Royal Beerain sat beside him. She was queen of her hive and considered a great beauty among the Insector. Those present knew her appearance hid a cold and deadly disposition. The last of the Big Four, Buguese, appeared nearly human, except for the antennae sprouting from his forehead. Buguese's clever, penetrating eyes gazed around the chamber, taking everything in. The other three knew he was constantly plotting, though whether his plots boded well or ill for the rest remained to be seen.

Mantid's meeting with the Big Four had barely begun when the door to the chamber swung open and Dungobeet entered. As usual, several message bugs buzzed around Mantid's servant. The Big Four regarded the smaller Insector with disdain.

"How dare he enter our meeting!" Beerain said haughtily. She looked at Dungobeet as though she might slay him on the spot.

Dungobeet veered away from her and bowed at the base of Mantid's platform. "I knew," he said, "that the master would want to hear of the latest developments."

"Concerning what?" Buguese asked.

"Concerning Centok and the...matter of Arachnian defense," Dungobeet replied, choosing his words carefully.

Mantid glared down at his servant. "Well?" he asked.

The short, beetle-like Insector bowed again. His bugs flitted nervously around the room. One flew too close to Stags, and the big Insector swatted it away with the back of his hand. The bug whipped across the room, hit the wall, and tumbled to the floor.

"Centok has decided to mount an all-out attack on the city," Dungobeet said.

"Can he do that?" Grasshop asked skittishly. "I thought that I would lead *my* swarms against the city—when we were ready."

"All will have their chance," Mantid said, his cold voice filling the chamber. "In time."

Buguese leaned back in his chair. "Centok seeks to win your favor, Mantid," he said lazily. "He seeks to join the ranks of the Big Four."

Stags stood and slammed his fists on the table. "There can only be four—and we are them!"

"We are *they*," Buguese corrected.

"Smart guy," Stags growled. "You're lucky I don't wipe that smile off your conceited face."

"Boys, boys, boys," Beerain said. "Are we here to fight among ourselves? Of course not!" She looked to the high platform. "Mantid will decide what is best. We are but his servants." The way she said it indicated that she didn't quite believe it.

Mantid rose. "Remember that, Beerain," he said, "if you wish to remain among the Big Four." As he spoke, the Big

Four settled back in their seats. Mantid looked at Dungobeet, who had gathered up his fallen message bug.

"Tell Centok that he has my permission to carry out his plan," Mantid said. "Their Oracle is shattered, and the city is nearly defenseless."

"I could have my troops there in fifteen sleeps!" Stags put in. "Why let this upstart gain the glory?"

Buguese shook his head and made a tsk-tsking sound. "Poor Stags," he said. "Big on muscles but not so big on brains." He smiled. "The master's plan is perfect. If Centok succeeds, our cause is won. If, on the other hand, he fails, we will learn more about the city defenses—which will help our next attack."

Mantid nodded and then spoke, his voice as cold as ice. "We will draw out the Turandot, find their weaknesses, and destroy them."

Hunter felt as though he were on a sleigh ride through barbed wire.

Leaves and brush whipped his skin as the rope pulled him through the jungle. He wrenched his fingers trying to free the looping knot that held his wrist tight. Already his whole body ached.

Hunter ducked and rolled, trying to avoid the trees and rocks whizzing by him as the big spider ran. About half the time he failed and slammed hard into some obstacle in their path. Spots danced before his eyes. He wished he'd never thought of this stupid plan.

The spider suddenly changed course. Hunter slammed into one final clump of prickly brush. Then he rocketed into the air. He looked up and saw that the spider was climbing the sheer face of the canyon.

"S-stop!" Hunter cried.

The spider either didn't hear him or didn't care. It kept going, almost straight up.

Hunter banged against the cliff face and some protruding scrub a couple of times. Overall, though, he preferred the climb to being dragged through the jungle. He stopped trying to free his wrist, as he didn't want to plummet back to the canyon bottom.

He held onto the rope with both hands, trying to take some of the pressure off his entangled wrist. The spider topped the cliff and ran across the rocky plain, taking Hunter with it.

Dust kicked up all around him, choking his lungs and stinging his eyes. He started to feel dizzy and weak. He made another attempt to free himself, but his fingers slipped numbly off the tangled knot.

Just when Hunter thought he would black out, the spider turned back toward him.

With one deft snip of its huge mandibles, it severed the rope around its leg.

Hunter skidded to a painful halt. He lay on his stomach, aching all over, as the dust settled around him. "I failed to catch a spider," he thought, "but at least I'm out of the canyon."

A huge shadow fell across him.

Hunter looked up and gazed into the red eyes of the titanic gray-black spider. He swallowed hard.

The spider reared, raising its six front legs and clashing its huge mandibles.

Hunter's heart froze. Not knowing what else to do, he blurted, "Sorry!"

The huge spider's legs crashed to the ground, pulverizing the earth beside Hunter's face.

"You *should* be sorry," echoed a voice in Hunter's head. "Very sorry, indeed. You are the most inept trainee I've ever seen."

Hunter looked around, unable to locate who was talking to him. "Igneous?" he ventured.

"Dim and rude as well as inept, I see," said the voice. "I knew you were trouble from the moment you first broke though the progenitor's web."

"Your progenitor's web?" Hunter asked, looking up at the spider. Amazingly, he didn't feel nearly as afraid as he would have been a few days ago.

"Yes," the spider replied, "in the cavern you fell through. Made an awful mess of Void's work, I must say. When I visited him shortly after, I hardly knew the place."

"*I* made a mess!" Hunter said angrily. He remembered his fear at being caught in the spider's web when he'd first fallen into Arachnia. So, he had been almost right. The spider he'd seen in that cave *was* related to this big spider. "Sorry I messed up your pal's web!" he thought. "I was fighting for my life at the time!"

The spider took a surprised step back. "Hmm," he said in Hunter's mind. "I heard that. Your mind talk's not bad, for a fool."

"Mind talk?" Hunter said.

"Forget it," the spider replied. "You've lost it now. Must have been dumb luck."

"I—I can still hear you," Hunter said.

105

The spider tilted his head. "Not hopeless, then. Just inept. Tell Igneous, or whomever you report to, that Darkness is not amused. Tell him not to send initiates out until they're ready. Good-bye."

With that, the spider turned away and headed for a group of rocky hills nearby.

Hunter sat up and rubbed his head, both to clear it and because it ached from his rough ride. "Good-bye!" he thought very hard.

The spider appeared not to hear him. It kept moving away, not at the fast gallop it had used when dragging him but at a leisurely pace.

Hunter felt incredibly stupid.

He sat quietly on the dusty ground for a moment. The blazing warmth of the Inner World sun pounded down on his scratched and scraped skin. He wondered, now that he was in the desert above the canyon, where he would find food and water. He had no idea which way to go to get back to Arachnia city.

And if he went back, what did he have to look forward to anyway? A life as a farmer? Hunter put his head in his hands and moped. As he did, a distant sound drifted to his ears.

At first he thought it was the noise of Darkness's legs, clattering over the rocky earth. Then he realized the sound was different from the noises that spiders made and it was coming from higher up, in the rocky hills ahead.

Hunter looked toward those hills. Darkness was ambling between two large spurs of rock. The big spider seemed tired, perhaps from pulling Hunter all over the canyon. Darkness didn't see or hear the Insectors lurking on the ridge above him.

The bugs looked like giant humanoid cockroaches. "Cockroach People," Hunter remembered Corona calling them. They waved their long antennae at one another and gestured toward the spider crawling in the valley below them. Hunter counted four or perhaps five of the bugs.

For a moment, he wondered what they might be up to. When they didn't run away from the approaching spider, Hunter realized their plan: they intended to ambush Darkness.

"Darkness!" Hunter called. "Look out!"

The big spider didn't hear him.

The cockroaches continued their preparations, arranging some kind of loosely woven netting along the top of the overlooking hills.

Hunter forgot his fears for a moment and ran toward the spider. "Darkness!" he cried again.

The cockroaches finished laying their trap. Those in front of the spider prepared to push boulders down in his path. Those behind readied what Hunter now recognized as a huge net.

Hunter remained too far away; the spider would never hear him. Darkness strolled toward his doom, unaware.

Hunter concentrated hard, trying with all his might to do the mind talk he'd done inadvertently earlier.

"Darkness! Look out!"

The big spider stopped and looked up, just as the cockroaches sprang their trap.

15
Shadow

Huge boulders rolled down the hill in front of the big gray-black spider.

Darkness sprang back, but that was just what the Cockroach People wanted. As the spider arced into the air, the roaches behind him threw their nets.

The ropy netting dropped over Darkness, entangling his body and legs. He fell to the ground, snared within the strands.

Hunter ran forward, his heart pounding. He didn't like spiders, but this spider had spared him, even after he'd rudely thrown a noose around its leg. He'd forced Darkness to climb out of the canyon, so in a way, this ambush was all Hunter's fault.

"Hey! Stop!" he cried, trying to get the roaches to pay attention to him.

But the Cockroach People knew their business. As Darkness thrashed within their net, they leaped down from the hills and threw more nets over him. Two of them rushed toward the spider's head with a heavy bag.

A purple dart flashed from Darkness's jaws, and one of the roaches went down. But the remaining roach dumped the contents of the bag on the spider. A cloud of greenish dust burst around Darkness's head.

The spider shrieked, a terrible sound.

In his head, Hunter heard, "*HELP!*"

The mind-talk cry nearly split Hunter's skull. He fell forward, clutching his hands to his temples. He felt dizzy and sick, as though someone had actually hit him in the head.

"I have to help," he thought. He forced his eyes open and willed himself to stand.

As he did, Darkness slumped to the ground, unmoving.

"No!" Hunter cried, unsure whether the spider was dead or merely unconscious.

The roaches noticed him for the first time.

Hunter drew his small knife as he came in on them. The Cockroach People turned and pelted him with rocks. Hunter brought his arms up to defend himself, but one of the stones slipped past his guard.

It hit Hunter on the side of the head, and the world exploded around him.

For a moment, everything was lights and flashing fireworks. Then everything went dark.

Hunter's head felt as though someone were beating a drum solo on it. A sour taste lingered in his mouth, and bells rang in his ears. Bright light streamed in through his eyelids, making the world seem red and angry.

Slowly, he opened his eyes. The world looked dazzlingly brilliant. For a moment, he hoped that his journey to the center of the earth had all been a bad dream.

Then a huge shadow fell over him.

The spider pounced before Hunter even had time to react. "What have you done with Darkness?" a deep voice boomed in his head.

Hunter tried to scramble away, but the spider surrounded him with its eight legs.

109

"Tell me!" it cried in his mind.

Fear shot through Hunter's aching body. Every time the new spider spoke, Hunter felt as if his head would split. The spider was in his mind!

"Get out!" Hunter cried. "Get out of my head!"

"What have you done with Darkness!"

Hunter felt as though a million tiny spiders were crawling all over his skin.

"GET OUT!" he thought as hard as he could.

The spider staggered, and Hunter rolled away from it, scrambling to his feet.

The spider was big and black. He'd seen it before, in the company of Darkness. The two arachnids often traveled through Spider Canyon together.

"What have you done with Darkness?" the spider said again. This time, its voice was a low growl in Hunter's mind. The spider crouched, as though it might spring on Hunter at any moment.

"I didn't do anything to Darkness," Hunter said, trying to think the words hard at the same time he said them.

"Where is he?"

"The roaches took him."

"Roaches?" The spider looked at Hunter suspiciously.

"Yes," Hunter said. "The roach people ambushed him and took him away. I tried to stop them, but they knocked me out."

"Why didn't they take you, too?"

"How do I know?" Hunter replied. "Maybe they thought I was dead."

"If you're lying to me, you'll wish you were dead," the spider said.

"I don't lie," Hunter thought firmly.

The spider rose from its crouch and circled Hunter, looking him over.

"Who are you, human?" the spider asked.

"I'm Hunter Steele, from the surface," he replied. "Who are you? Is Darkness your father?"

The spider hissed suspiciously in Hunter's mind.

"Cut that out," Hunter said. "I answered your question. Now you answer mine."

"I'm Shadow the Untamed," the spider replied. "Darkness is my elder. If you've done anything to him..."

"Will you get it through your thick carapace that I had nothing to do with this!"

"Somehow," the spider said, eyeing Hunter suspiciously, "I doubt that."

Hunter tried not to think about lassoing Darkness with his rope.

"You did what?" Shadow asked indignantly.

Hunter realized he'd have to try harder not to think around this spider. "I'm going to be a Spider Rider," he mind-talked. "I was sent to catch my own spider."

"That's ridiculous," Shadow said. "No one *catches* a spider. Who sent you?"

"Prince Lumen," Hunter replied.

The spider bobbed his head agitatedly. "Yes," he said, "that might be possible. The prince has much to learn." He turned to leave, following tracks left by the roaches.

"Where are you going," Hunter asked.

"To rescue Darkness," Shadow replied.

"Then I'm going, too."

"Why?"

"Because," Hunter said, "he could have killed me for trying to catch him, and he didn't."

"Then be happy and go home," Shadow said.

"Darkness never would have left the canyon if not for me," Hunter said. "So I kind of owe him." In his deepest thoughts, Hunter wondered if perhaps Darkness—whose master, Void, lived in the tunnel in the sky—might be able to show him the way home. Hunter was very careful to shield this thought from Shadow, though.

"There's something you're not telling me," Shadow said. "What is it?"

"Nothing important," Hunter replied.

The spider turned back on him and glared. "If you're trying to trap me," Shadow said, "you'll regret it."

"That's the last thing I want," Hunter said truthfully. "I just want to help Darkness and go home."

"Very well, then," Shadow said. "Try to keep up." He turned and began walking again, searching for clues in the tracks as he went.

"Aren't you going to let me ride you?" Hunter asked.

"No one rides me, boy," Shadow replied. "I have never taken a rider and never will. That's what *untamed* means." He kept going.

Legs aching, Hunter trudged after him.

The two hardly thought a word to each other all during their trek. The desert remained hard and rocky. Hunter soon used up the water in his canteen. With food plentiful in the canyon, he hadn't thought to bring any with him on his hunts.

As the unblinking sun beat down on them, Hunter began to grow hungry, thirsty, and tired. He looked enviously at the giant spider. Shadow never seemed to thirst or tire.

Waves of heat washed over the rocky landscape. More than once, Hunter imagined he saw water, but it was only a mirage, a trick of the heat.

"Keep your mind focused or you'll die," Shadow scolded.

"You'd just let me die out here?" Hunter mind-talked back.

"I didn't want you along in the first place," the spider replied.

Hunter didn't remember passing out. But when he woke again, he was by the side of a pool in an oasis at the desert's edge. He felt water dripping against his face and saw one of Shadow's black legs arcing over him. Water dripped off the spider's armor and onto Hunter's face.

Hunter sputtered, fear and disgust mixing in his belly.

"That's fine, thanks," the spider said in his mind.

Hunter scooped some water from the pool and drank. "I thought you didn't care if I died," Hunter said. "Why did you rescue me, then?"

"I didn't want you to become food for the scorpions," Shadow replied. "I hate scorpions. There are too many of them in the world."

"Too many spiders, too," Hunter thought, doing his best to keep the idea from Shadow.

The spider flicked its leg and dumped Hunter into the pool.

Hunter sat up in the shallow water and sputtered, "What did you do that for?"

"I thought maybe there were too many humans in this world," the spider said. "Or, at least, too many *dry* humans."

"Very funny," Hunter said. He stood up and wrung out his clothes, trying hard not to mentally curse out the spider as he did so.

After he'd dried off, had something to drink, and had rested awhile, Hunter felt a lot less angry. As calmly as he could, he asked, "Where are we?"

"Close to the cockroach nest," Shadow replied. "But the trail has grown cold. You wasted too much time."

"Well, pardon me for passing out." Hunter got the impression that the spider didn't forgive him. "So, what's the plan?" he asked.

"How should I know?" Shadow said. "Plans are for humans."

"Well," Hunter said, "I guess we should scout the area, discover where the nest entrances are. Then maybe we can find a clue to where they're keeping Darkness."

"All right," Shadow agreed.

The oasis stood at the edge of another lush Arachnian forest. Thick underbrush covered the forest floor. Hunter was sweating within minutes from trying to push through it.

"I don't think the roaches came this way," he said.

"I know they're around here somewhere," Shadow replied. "I can smell them."

"It would be a lot quicker going if I rode on your back," Hunter said. He didn't particularly want to ride on the spider, but he *did* want to get this errand over as quickly as he could.

"I told you," Shadow said, his thoughts cold and hostile, "I won't take a rider."

"Yeah, yeah," Hunter said. "Be proud. That's the best way to help your friend."

The coarse hairs along Shadow's back prickled, but the spider didn't reply.

"Can't you spiders speak telepathically to one another or something?" Hunter asked.

"Yes," Shadow replied peevishly. "But only when we're awake."

"So you think Darkness is unconscious or..."

"I won't think about it," Shadow's mind barked. "There could be other reasons I don't hear him...any number of things."

"Meaning he could be dead already," Hunter thought, trying *not* to be heard.

"I told you not to think that!" Shadow snapped.

Hunter pushed his way past another prickly bush. "Okay, okay," he thought. "Keep the noise down!"

Then, without warning, three huge shapes jumped down on them from the trees.

16
Nest of the Roach

Hunter hit the ground hard. Shadow spun, hissing and rearing, ready to fight.

"I don't believe it," said a familiar human voice.

Hunter scrambled to his feet and found himself looking at the point end of Magma's lance.

"And we thought this noisy pair must be roaches!" Magma said. His was the voice that had first spoken.

Corona laughed. "You said we'd never see him again, Igneous!" she chided.

Igneous folded his arms over his muscular chest. "Clearly, I was mistaken," he said. "This Earthen is apparently steel in more than name."

Shadow looked from the three riders and their spiders to Hunter. "You're *Earthen*?" Shadow said. "Well, that figures. Disaster seems to trail in your wake."

"What are you doing here, Earthen?" Igneous asked. "And is this the spider you've bonded with?" He rubbed his chin. "It *might* be a good match."

"*No*," Hunter and Shadow both said quickly.

"We're not together," the spider explained. The Spider Riders clearly heard him. All three of them laughed.

"Unlikely companions, then," Corona said. "Up into the trees with you both. We're hunting roaches, and we don't want to be seen."

With that, Venus, Brutus, and Flame shot webs and quickly ascended back into the treetops.

Shadow shot a web and climbed up after them.

"Hey!" Hunter called up from below. "What about me?"

"I'm not your keeper," the spider replied in his mind.

"No one's asking you to be," Hunter replied. "But if I don't climb up, it'll ruin the plan."

Shadow shot out a web line to Hunter. Before he could grab it, the line snagged him by the ankle. Shadow gave a tremendous yank, and Hunter zoomed into the air like a snared rabbit. The spider reeled him in and set him down in the treetop. Hunter brushed off the web line and tried to keep from falling.

"Keep yourselves concealed," Igneous whispered to both of them.

Shadow had no trouble hiding amid the slender branches and leaves, but Hunter had a hard time keeping his balance.

"Not very good at this, are you?" Shadow said.

"I bet you're not very good at snowboarding or video games," Hunter replied.

"What's a so-boring idiot-game?" Shadow asked.

"It's just that some of us are better at some things than others," Hunter said. He turned to Corona. "Psst! Corona," he called. "Why are you hunting roaches? Does it have something to do with the next shard?"

"Keep it down, will you?" Igneous said angrily. "Do you want the roaches to hear? Use mind talk."

"Corona," Hunter thought, "what's the story?"

"She can't hear you," Shadow mind-talked back. "She can hear only her spider in mind talk. Didn't they teach you anything at the rider academy?"

"I didn't go to the rider academy, for your information," Hunter replied. "I'm Earthen, remember? I just got here."

The spider remained expressionless, but Hunter got the feeling he was frowning. "Venus says they're hunting for the next shard—whatever that is. The other spiders don't seem pleased that you've guessed this. They say you're an outsider and don't belong here. I agree with them."

"Terrific," Hunter said. "What else do they say?"

"They believe the shard to be in the roach nest. I just told Venus and the others that the roaches have taken Darkness and we're here to free him. The other spiders are angry and want to help us."

"Well, that's good, I guess," Hunter thought.

Shadow said nothing for a long while as they lurked in the treetops. The riders grew impatient waiting for a roach to come to them. They had planned to ambush one and force him to tell about the nest.

When none came quickly, Igneous and Flame slipped away on a scouting mission. Igneous commanded the rest to stay behind and await his return.

"Hunter," Shadow finally said in mind talk, "the other spiders have explained about the shard to me. They wanted us to leave, but I have convinced them that we can help. I told them we won't leave until we free Darkness. They've agreed to this."

"Again, I say, 'terrific,'" Hunter replied.

Just then, Igneous returned.

"Flame says they found the nest," Shadow explained. "He says to follow him and stay quiet."

"What about Darkness?" Hunter asked.

"They don't know," Shadow replied. "But we'll find him." The big spider looked at Hunter. "Climb on my back," he said. "But *don't* get used to it."

Hunter climbed up and clung precariously to Shadow as they followed Igneous to the nest.

The roach nest looked pretty much like the rest of the jungle to Hunter. Only when he looked carefully could he make out the mass of tangled foliage that formed the lair.

Corona and Venus drew close to Hunter and Shadow. "The nest entrance is narrow," Corona whispered. "We'll have to go in on foot."

"I'm okay with that," Hunter said. Getting off the back of the spider seemed good to him.

"Do you have a weapon?" she asked.

"Only the knife you gave me," he said.

"Do you want my sword?" she asked.

"I'd do better with a club," Hunter said. "I swing a mean baseball bat in school."

Shadow snapped off a stout tree branch just the size and weight of a regulation bat and gave it to him.

"Thanks," Hunter said, almost meaning it.

"The spiders will wait outside for us," Corona explained. "They'll listen and help when they can. Are you confident in your mind talk?"

"Sure," Hunter lied.

"Let's go, then," she said.

Shadow and the other spiders let out a web line, and the riders slid down from the trees. Hunter nearly fell while climbing down his line, but he caught himself and made it safely to the ground.

Igneous led them down what appeared to be a game trail to an opening in the densely packed foliage.

"A side door to the nest," he explained. "I overpowered the guard and webbed him nearby. Remember, though we want to free Darkness, recovering the shard is our primary mission. Stay together. If something happens, and we get split up, we'll meet back here."

"Think you can find this exit again, Earthen?" Magma asked.

"Worry about yourself, hotshot," Hunter replied.

Magma chuckled.

Cautiously, the four of them moved into the roach nest.

To Hunter, it looked a little like a corn maze he'd once visited back home—except there was a ceiling overhead, and the corn was actually random bits of plant matter. It appeared to be held together with some kind of sticky goo.

"Roach saliva," Shadow said in his mind. "Looks pretty fresh, too." Hunter almost jumped out of his sneakers.

"Don't do that!" he said mentally.

"Do what?"

"Sneak into my mind like that when I can't see you," Hunter replied.

"I have to," Shadow said. "You're my key to finding Darkness."

"Well, don't do it without warning me," Hunter said.

"You're warned," Shadow shot back. "I'm doing it all the ti..." But the thought faded away.

Hunter looked around nervously. He wasn't very good at mind talk yet, but the spider's absence bothered him more than he would have admitted.

Ahead, the tunnel opened up slightly. Green light filtered in from above, relieving a bit of the oppressive darkness.

"Careful," Igneous whispered.

As he said it, the walls around them gave way and a half dozen roach warriors leaped into their midst.

17
The Second Shard

"Ambush!" Magma cried.

Hunter brought his makeshift club up barely in time to ward off the claw of an attacking roach. Apparently, the Cockroach People had lain in wait for them, hidden behind false walls in the tunnel. Since the tunnels seemed to be composed mainly of trash and bracken, the trap had been undetectable.

The roach's claw skidded off Hunter's club. Hunter clouted the Insector in the head, and the roach fell back. Two more rushed forward to take his place.

"They must have known we were coming!" Magma said over the din of the fighting. He and the other riders drew their swords and defended themselves against the roach attack. The roaches outnumbered them more than three to one.

"But how?" Corona asked. She smashed her fist between the eyes of a roach, while fending off its claws with her sword.

"Maybe we made too much noise," Magma suggested. He shot a brief, accusing glance toward Hunter. The mercenary sidestepped the thrust of a roach spear. Before the roach recovered, Magma clouted it on the back of the brainpan with the hilt of his sword. The roach sprawled to the floor.

"It doesn't matter," Igneous said. "Focus on the mission. Together, now." As one, the three riders swung toward the main body of the attacking roaches.

Shadow's voice, dim and distant from outside the nest, echoed in Hunter's mind. "Fire your energy weapon with the rest of them," the spider said.

"I don't have an energy weapon," Hunter thought back.

"Figures," the spider sniffed.

"HIZZ-AHHH!" Magma cried as he, Corona, and Igneous fired. Blasts of energy seared from their silver manacles. The shots burst into the main column of the roaches, bowling them over.

"This way," Igneous cried, dashing through the gap in their enemies. He ran across the chamber at the end of the tunnel and headed for an exit at the far side of the room.

Corona and Magma sprinted after him. Hunter started to follow, but before he could reach the exit on the far side of the chamber, a roach rose out of the tangled pile of stunned bodies and tackled him.

Hunter fell back, smashing into a wall. The wall gave way, tumbling trash and compost down on top of him. He grabbed a handful of the garbage and threw it in the roach's eyes.

The roach screeched and shook its head. Hunter kicked it in the gut, and it fell away from him. Hunter scrambled to his feet. He backed into the passage formed by the new hole in the wall. "Corona! Igneous!" he cried. "Help!" But the Spider Riders seemed to be out of earshot.

The roaches in the chamber shook off the blast effects and rose to their feet once more. They stood between Hunter and the exit the others had taken. There were far too many Insectors for Hunter to tackle on his own. The roaches advanced, their hideous mouth parts clicking and hissing.

Hunter turned and ran. The tunnel around him was damp and gloomy. Only tiny rays of greenish light drifted in through the rotting vegetation of the ceiling.

He passed one passageway on the left leading deeper into the gloom, then another on the right, leading back the way he'd last seen his friends. Hunter took the second turn and kept going.

"Corona! Igneous! Magma!" he cried.

The only sound that came back was the distant clicking of the roach horde. Hunter's spine went cold. He was trapped here, in the middle of a huge bug nest, with no clear idea where his friends were or how to get out.

He approached another chamber on the right. Something inside it glittered warm and red. He started to enter, but as he did, he spotted two cockroach guards. They stood inside the chamber, in front of the glowing object. The roaches' bodies prevented Hunter from seeing what the thing was.

The roaches turned toward him. Both wore heavy armor and carried wicked-looking barbed spears.

"Sorry, wrong turn!" Hunter said. He swerved and kept running down the corridor.

"Klak-kai hai!" one of the roaches shouted.

Hunter didn't dare look back, but the sound of roach feet pursuing him echoed dimly in the cluttered corridor.

"Roklo ka!" a raspy voice shouted.

Hunter turned and saw one roach guard a dozen paces behind him. The guard threw his spear at him.

Hunter ducked aside just in time. The spear's barbs sliced

through the front of his shirt, barely missing the skin. The weapon lodged in the wall next to him.

Hunter grabbed the spear's shaft and pulled. He grunted as the weapon remained stuck in the wall.

The roach cackled and moved in on him, whirling its razor-sharp foreclaws.

Hunter's heart pounded. Fear froze his legs in place.

The face of the giant insect looked like a hideous fright mask. Sticky drool dripped from its mouth. Hunter fumbled for his club.

The roach swung its right arm at him. Hunter brought the club up. The roach's claw smashed into the wood, gouging it like an ax. Splinters dashed against Hunter's face, and he blinked to keep the fragments out of his eyes.

The roach hissed and swung its left arm.

A thorny-shafted Spider Rider lance streaked past Hunter's left shoulder. The roach's blow struck it and skidded off, missing the boy.

"Hunter, duck!" Corona cried.

Hunter did as he was told. His knees buckled, and he flattened himself against the wall.

Corona stepped past him, twisting her lance as she came. The lance clouted the roach on the side of the head.

The Insector staggered. As it did, Corona whirled. She put her lance against the back of the roach's neck and forced it to the ground. The giant bug hit the earth with a grunt.

Before it could rise again, Corona leaped forward and grabbed a circular disk on the back of its neck. With one quick twist, she removed the guard's life force medallion. The roach dissolved into sticky brown mist and seeped into Corona's trophy.

Hunter got to his feet. "How'd you find me?" he asked.

"Shadow told Venus you were in trouble, and she told me," Corona said. "I was lucky to find you. The spiders said your thoughts were very jumbled."

"Were they ever!" Hunter agreed.

"If you're going to be a rider, you *must* learn to concentrate," Corona cautioned. "Our bond with our spiders is our main advantage over the Insectors."

"Where are the others?" Hunter asked.

"We're supposed to make our way back to the entrance and..." Corona paused. "Quiet," she said.

"Found him...," Shadow's voice said in Hunter's mind. The spider sounded very distant and indistinct.

"Found who?" Hunter asked.

"Darkness," Corona said. "Venus says Igneous and Magma have located him. This way." Without waiting to see if Hunter was following, she darted down the corridor, back the way she'd come.

With a mighty pull, Hunter yanked the roach spear from the wall. Then he hurried after her. He left his ruined club behind.

Hunter could barely follow the twists and turns as they raced through the maze of cockroach passages. Corona seemed to know where she was going, though. In all the Inner World, she was the only one—human or spider—that Hunter truly trusted.

"Get ready to fight," she said as they rounded a corner. Her power manacle hummed as she dashed into the room ahead.

Inside, Igneous and Magma were fighting seven roach guards. Darkness lay in the middle of the room, pinned down by netting spiked into the ground.

"I'll help the others," Corona instructed. "You cut Darkness free."

"Check," Hunter said. He repressed a shudder at the sight of the huge spider and ran forward.

"Duck!" Shadow's faint voice said in his mind.

Hunter ducked as a lightning bolt from Corona seared over his head. The blast hit a roach that had been about to jump him. The roach twirled through the air and crashed to the ground.

Hunter dashed past the fallen Insector to Darkness's side. He slashed at the netting with his borrowed spear. He heard the deep voice of Darkness in his mind.

"Good to see you, Earthen," the spider said. "Something of a surprise, as well. I thought you didn't like spiders."

Hunter paused, a bit embarrassed that Darkness had seen the arachnophobia in his mind. "I had to help you," he said. "It was kind of my fault you got caught." He finished cutting the last of the main tethers.

Darkness stood and ripped himself free.

The three roaches still on their feet froze in fear. The older spider quickly knocked two of them out, while Magma incapacitated the third.

"Let's go!" Igneous said. A number of corridors led out of the big prison chamber, but only one of them was large enough for a spider. The three riders, Hunter, and Darkness ran down it.

"What about the shard?" Corona called. Ahead of them, daylight peeked through the rotting walls.

"We'll have to come back for it another time," Igneous replied. "With the nest stirred up like this, we've no chance to recover it now."

Suddenly, Hunter remembered something. "The shard!" he said.

"What about it?" Magma asked.

"I saw it when I was running from the roaches!"

"That's not very likely," Igneous said.

Hunter concentrated with all his might. "Have your spiders ask Shadow," he said. "I'm making a mental picture for him of what I saw."

The others all paused a moment to listen to their spider mounts.

"Hunter is right," Corona said. "Venus and the other spiders agree."

"Where was it?" Igneous asked.

"Back near where Corona rescued me from the bug guard," Hunter said. "I think I can find it again."

"I'll go with him," Corona offered.

They reached the end of the tunnel. The roaches had partially blocked the exit with vegetation to conceal it. Darkness threw his bulk against the barricade, and it crumbled away. Light streamed into the nest from outside.

"All right," Igneous said, "you go. If you don't make it, we'll try a rescue once things settle down."

"Don't worry about us," Corona said. "Worry about the shard. C'mon, Hunter."

"Good luck, Earthen," Darkness called in his mind.

The Earth boy and the Turandot girl dashed back into the roach lair. Worry nagged at Hunter's guts. What if they ran into more of the roaches? What if he couldn't find the shard again?

"Fine time to mention that...," Shadow's voice said faintly in his mind.

"Keep your thoughts to yourself!" Hunter mind-talked back. He heard the distant clattering of roach warriors but couldn't tell from which direction the noises came. He and Corona raced through the big prison chamber and back into the adjoining corridor, retracing their steps.

"Now where?" Corona asked.

"Back the way I came," Hunter said, hoping he was leading her in the right direction. "The roach you fought was guarding the shard."

"Were there more?" she asked.

"One other," he replied. "Maybe more by now."

Corona nodded grimly. "Fight your best," she said.

He nodded back and took the lead.

A few minutes later they reached the turn in the corridor where he'd seen the chamber. "That's it!" he said.

"Mind-talk now," she cautioned. "The roaches may be listening."

"But—" Hunter began.

"Shh!" Corona hissed.

She inched ahead of him toward the chamber doorway. Glittering, reddish light leaked from inside. She cautiously peered into the room, then backed away. She grinned and nodded.

"...doesn't...any...inside...," Shadow's voice said faintly in Hunter's mind.

"What?" Hunter thought. "Mind-talk louder."

Corona stepped into the room.

A flash of movement from the doorway caught Hunter's eye.

"Corona, look out!" Hunter's mind screamed.

She didn't hear him, though, and stepped right into the path of the descending stinger.

18
Shadow and Darkness

The giant scorpion's stinger flashed through the air and bit through Corona's armor, into her shoulder.

Corona stared at the stinger for a moment in disbelief. The scorpion's tail whipped back, leaving an arcing trail of black venom as it withdrew.

Corona's sword flashed, and the tip of the stinger fell from the scorpion's tail. The injured creature backed up into the shard chamber. A huge, hideous roach sat on its back.

Hunter leaped to Corona's side. Wounded, Corona staggered back as the scorpion came at her again. It snapped with its huge, sharp-edged pincers. Corona parried one claw with her sword but wasn't fast enough to stop the other. She looked woozy and weak.

Hunter thrust his spear at the claw and forced it aside. The pincer snapped shut on thin air, missing Corona.

She flashed Hunter a smile, trying to hide the pain of her wound. "Aim for the bare spot under the scorpion's chin," she said. "A blow there will paralyze the beast."

The scorpion and rider came at them again. Hunter and Corona parried, fending off the claws once more. Behind the roach warrior and his steed, a glowing gemlike shard rested on a waist-high pedestal. A cage of thick tree branches surrounded the treasure.

Hunter lunged forward, aiming his spear for a less-armored spot under the scorpion's mouth. The black scorpion skittered backward, slashing at Hunter with its pincers. The roach on its back stabbed at Hunter with a jagged spear.

Hunter stepped aside, barely in time. The spear got caught in his torn shirt. The roach pulled the weapon back. The force of it yanked Hunter off his feet. The roach twisted the spear free and prepared to stab Hunter again.

"L-lightning lance!" Corona shouted.

White electricity blazed from her power manacle and smashed into the roach's chest. The roach flew off its mount and crashed into the cage containing the shard. The wooden bars smashed, and the shard tumbled to the floor. The roach fell beside it, unconscious.

The loss of its master disoriented the scorpion. Hunter quickly drove his spear up into the unprotected spot under the monster's chin. The scorpion reeled sideways and fell paralyzed beside the roach.

Hunter glanced at Corona and smiled. They were home free! The scorpion rider was the only roach in the chamber. Hunter grabbed the shard and tucked the precious crystal into his pants pocket.

Corona smiled back at him, then wobbled and fell face-first onto the floor.

"Corona!" Hunter gasped.

He raced to his friend's side and lifted her to her feet. Her eyelids fluttered slightly, and the power crystal on her manacle flashed dimly. When she had passed out, her weapons had been absorbed back into her armor.

Hunter tried to think. Did he know the way out of the lair by himself? Maybe. It would be tough carrying Corona, though.

He concentrated and thought hard. "Shadow!" he called. "Darkness! Corona's hurt! We need help!" No reply came.

A rustling sound from the other side of the shard chamber caught his attention. He turned and saw two more warrior roaches entering the room.

"Time to go," Hunter said, knowing Corona couldn't hear him. He half carried, half dragged her out of the room.

"Kroka-ka!" the roaches clacked.

Hunter kept going as fast as he could. He didn't have to look to know the roaches were already on his heels. Corona's legs stumbled along as they went, but she wasn't really conscious.

The stinger wound in her shoulder oozed black poison. She'd grown very, very pale. "Help!" Hunter called. "Help!"

The roaches behind them cackled.

Hunter lugged Corona around a corner, and his heart froze. Ahead of them stood two scorpion-mounted roach warriors, blocking the main tunnel. A small side passage led off to the left. Hunter thought he saw light at the end of it.

He dragged Corona into the narrow space, hoping the scorpions, at least, wouldn't be able to follow.

The passageway grew progressively tighter as they went. One of the unmounted roaches came in after them.

Hunter stabbed at the roach's face with his spear. The creature blinked and backed away, beyond Hunter's reach. The scorpion riders stepped forward. With a clacking and slashing of claws, the evil giant scorpions began to dig, expanding the tunnel, making it large enough for the roach guards to enter two abreast.

Sweat poured down Hunter's body. Fear clutched at his gut. He kept backpedaling, taking Corona with him. She mumbled deliriously. Her legs stopped working entirely. Hunter was forced to drag her, which slowed them down even more.

"C'mon, Corona!" he said. "C'mon! Wake up!"

The roaches and the scorpions let out a horrible, hissing sound. With the tunnel wide enough to admit them, they advanced. The scorpions came in front with the other roach warriors to the rear.

Hunter backed into something. He looked over his shoulder, and his heart fell even further. He'd reached the end of the tunnel! The light he'd seen wasn't an exit; it was just a small hole in the matted, rotting foliage of the wall. He and Corona were trapped!

He put the injured girl behind him and faced their enemies. Hunter's "borrowed" spear seemed scant protection against the claws of the advancing scorpions. If the roaches hadn't had to dig through the garbage to reach him, he'd probably have been dead already.

Hunter gritted his teeth and prepared for the final battle of his life. He glanced at the power manacle on Corona's arm, wishing he knew how to use it. Would it even work for him? Too late to find out now.

The scorpions ripped through the final few feet of tunnel wall separating them. Hunter stabbed at the monsters with his spear. The scorpions batted the blade aside with their pincers. Hunter barely managed to hold onto the weapon. The scorpions raised their deadly tails to strike.

Hunter held his breath and waited. He knew he couldn't stop two stings at once. The passage seemed to shake with the pounding of his heart.

But it wasn't his heart—the passage actually *was* shaking!

Suddenly, giant mandibles tore through the roof over the scorpion riders' heads and ripped it off. Light streamed in from outside. The riders backed up as a giant spider fell into their midst. The garbage that composed the roach nest's walls rolled off the spider's gray-black carapace.

"Darkness!" Hunter gasped.

The giant spider leaped at the nearest scorpion. The scorpion and its rider fell back as Darkness sprayed them with sticky webbing.

The second scorpion lashed at Darkness with its stinger. Hunter lunged forward and blocked the blow with his lance. The roach warriors stood stunned at their sudden misfortune. They glanced from the titanic spider to each other, unsure whether to attack or run.

"Well parried, Earthen," Darkness said in the boy's mind. "Thank you."

"How did you find me?" Hunter asked.

"You called," Darkness explained.

"I thought nobody heard," Hunter said.

"The others didn't, but I did," Darkness said.

The scorpion came at him again. The elder spider kicked it back with six legs. The bug and rider tumbled across the room and crashed onto their sides. The scorpion rolled to its feet; its rider kept his saddle.

"What about the others?" Hunter asked.

The roach warriors regained their courage and charged. Hunter fended them off with his spear. He didn't know how long he could hold them, though.

"Venus heard Corona's cry," Darkness replied. "She and Shadow are coming. The others, too, as quickly as they can. The whole nest is massing against us. *Argh!*"

The spider's cry shot through Hunter's mind like a blow to the head. As Darkness was fighting one scorpion, the other had cut itself free of the webs. It stung the great spider in the side. Darkness hadn't seen it coming.

"No!" Hunter cried. He sprang forward, bulling his way past the roach warriors. He stabbed the attacking scorpion under the chin, and it went limp. "Darkness!" he thought urgently. "Are you all right?"

"It is ... only a scratch," the spider replied.

Though the second scorpion had fallen, its roach rider remained unscathed. The roach dismounted and attacked Hunter with a serrated-edged sword.

Hunter fell back, parrying with his spear. The other two roach warriors moved to surround him.

Darkness lunged into the middle of them. "Get out!" he cried in Hunter's mind. "Take the girl and go!"

"How?" Hunter asked. The hole the spider had made in the nest's roof was well above his head.

"Climb up my back," Darkness said.

"But—" Hunter began.

"I can hold them off," Darkness said. "They are no match for me."

Hunter didn't know whether to believe the old spider or not. He sensed something uneasy in the arachnid's telepathic tone.

"Do it now!" Darkness ordered.

Hunter grabbed Corona and dragged her toward the hole. Darkness extended him a leg, and Hunter scrambled up the spider's back, pulling Corona after him. All the while, Darkness kept fending off the roach warriors.

More roaches swarmed in, and more, and more. They

came with spears and swords and lances and bows. Some rode scorpions. They filled the newly hewn chamber, expanding it by cutting through the walls as they came.

Darkness raised his body up as high as he could for Hunter to reach the escape hole. The gigantic spider stood on two legs and fended off the incoming roaches with his other six appendages.

Hunter reached for the roof of the roach nest. His fingers slipped, just missing the edge. The spider lurched, and Corona almost fell off his back. Hunter grabbed her just in time.

"We can't make it!" he cried, tiring both mentally and physically. "I can't reach!"

Darkness didn't reply immediately. He was too busy fighting off the roach hordes, which now outnumbered him a hundred to one. The Insectors stabbed and sliced at him. Their scorpions stung the spider's enormous body. The Insectors tried to reach Hunter and the unconscious Corona, but Darkness would not let them.

The spider whirled his armored legs, slashing at the bugs, driving them back.

Hunter tried again, reaching desperately for the ledge just above his head. Two ominous shadows fell across the opening.

"Shadow!" Hunter cried. "Venus!"

The two spiders crouched near the opening and fired their webs. In an instant, they ensnared Hunter and Corona and pulled the young warriors to safety.

"Help Darkness!" Hunter told the spiders, thinking as hard as he could. He clung desperately to Shadow's back.

The two spiders quickly enlarged the opening in the roof

and leaped down next to their comrade. Darkness moved slowly now. Dozens of wounds pierced his armored hide.

Venus and Shadow hurled themselves into the roaches, scattering the bugs like tenpins. In moments, they cleared an area around their wounded friend.

Darkness and Shadow looked at each other. "I will get you out, my elder," Hunter heard Shadow say to the older spider.

His strength nearly gone, Darkness could only nod.

Working together, Venus and Shadow sprayed a wall of webs between themselves and the roaches. Then they wove a quick net around their wounded comrade. As one, the spiders sprang through the hole in the roof, taking Hunter, Corona, and Darkness with them.

The roof of the roach nest quaked with their weight as they quickly moved away from the breach. "Are you all right, boy?" Shadow asked in Hunter's mind.

"I'm okay," Hunter said. "How's Corona?"

"Venus is unsure," the spider replied. "She is very worried about her."

Hunter nodded. He felt worried, too, both for Corona and for Darkness. The old spider limped along, almost being carried by Venus and Shadow.

Behind them, the roaches and their scorpions swarmed out of the hole in the roof. Worry clenched Hunter's gut. Slowed down by Darkness, he doubted they could stay ahead of the bugs for very long.

"HIZZ-AHHH!" The Spider Rider war cry echoed through the humid air.

Magma and Igneous riding Brutus and Flame stormed toward them over the nest's roof. They sped past the departing spiders and crashed into the column of advancing roaches.

Bugs fell by the dozens as Igneous and Magma laid into them with lance, sword, and manacle energy weapons. The roaches fell back. The Spider Riders quickly refocused their attacks on the nest roof, weakening the rotting vegetation. The roof gave way under the roaches. The spiders and their riders sprang back, avoiding the collapse.

They turned and raced back to join the rest.

Working together, the spiders soon reached the rocky highlands beyond the roaches' forest country. They stopped atop a high hill to rest.

"They won't be catching us here," Magma said, looking toward the jungle far below. "How's Corona?"

Igneous knelt by her side. Corona was very pale, and her breath came in shallow gasps. The hole in her armor where she'd been stung oozed black venom. "The poison is bad," Igneous said. "But I think my manacle has enough power to help."

He laid his hands on Corona's head and shoulders. The silver bracelet on his wrist began to glow. The blue-white light spread through the manacle into Igneous's hands, then to Corona. Soon, the glow surrounded all of the injured Spider Rider's body.

Gradually, the color returned to her face and the wound in her shoulder stopped oozing. Corona took a deep breath and moaned, as if waking from a long sleep.

Hunter sighed with relief.

Igneous slumped over, exhausted from the effort. "She'll live," he said.

"But what about Darkness?" Hunter asked. He looked from Corona to the brave spider, lying nearby. Shadow, Venus, Brutus, and Flame stood near their comrade, stroking him with their many legs and clicking consolingly.

Igneous rose and gazed at his manacle. The power gems embedded in it blinked weakly, the same as the crystals in Corona's bracelet. "I don't know," Igneous said. "I'm not expert at healing spiders. And my manacle is almost depleted."

"Mine's running low, too," Magma said. "But I'll lend you the power if you think it might help."

"Me, too," Corona said, opening her eyes. Hunter helped her stand, and all four of them went to the injured spider.

The Spider Riders linked their hands, and Igneous tried the healing power. The blue-white glow spread from the lead rider's hands to the elder arachnid. But the power sputtered and died. Darkness's body seemed too large, or perhaps his wounds were too terrible, for the healing glow to fix.

Igneous hung his head and stepped back. The others did as well.

Hunter looked from one rider to the next. He didn't much like spiders, but *this* spider had saved his life.

"Can't you do anything for him?" Hunter asked, tears budding at the corners of his eyes.

"The power of the manacles isn't enough," Igneous said. "If we can get him back to the city..."

"I will not survive...that long." Darkness's thoughts echoed in Hunter's mind and the minds of the others. "But there is something I must do," the ancient spider said. "Shadow, come here."

The jet-black arachnid came to his elder's side and lowered his head close to the wounded spider's eyes. "Yes, my elder?" Shadow said.

"This boy—this Hunter—risked his life to save me," Darkness gasped. The gray-black spider's voice sounded frail and distant now. "There is something...special in him. You and he will make a great team...in time."

"Team?" Shadow said indignantly. "I will have no rider—neither this boy nor anyone else. I am untamed!"

"Untamed...but now...partnered," Darkness said. "It is...my final...request...." The light went out of his eyes, and the great spider moved no more.

"I...," Shadow began. His bright golden eyes dimmed slightly. He looked from his elder to the Earthen boy. Hunter fought back tears.

Shadow hung his head over his fallen friend. The black spider's mind talk sounded very softly in Hunter's head. "Yes," Shadow said. "I will do as you ask, my elder."

PART THREE

THE BATTLE FOR ARACHNIA

19
A New Rider

Prince Lumen gazed at the floor and shook his head sadly. "That's terrible news," he said. "Very terrible. Darkness was a great spider—elder to many of the best spiders ever in the corps. Surely that is why the roaches captured him, to try to gain an advantage over his kin."

The prince paced nervously around the command room of the Spider Rider corps. His sister, Princess Sparkle, followed a few steps behind him. The riders had returned to the city less than an hour earlier. Igneous, Magma, Corona, and Hunter all stood at attention, listening to the prince. Their spiders waited outside in the spider paddocks.

To Hunter it seemed like years since he'd been dropped off in Spider Canyon. He still felt sick inside over what had happened to Darkness. Hunter had never thought he would like a spider, never mind admire one. But Darkness had given up his life for a human boy and a Turandot girl. That was a debt Hunter could never repay.

Lumen took a deep breath. "We've paid a high price to gain our prize," he said. He held his hand out to Igneous. "Where is the shard?"

The Spider Rider commander took a deep breath. "Lost, my prince," he said.

The prince and princess gasped as though struck.

"We could not recover it," Igneous explained. "The battle to save Darkness and then rescue our own people.... It became too much. We had to leave the shard behind."

"We'll go back," Corona offered, "as soon as the nest settles. I've seen the shard and—"

"Wait a minute," Hunter said. "I've got it. It's right here." He reached into his pants pocket and pulled out the glittering gem. He'd gotten so wrapped up in his worries about Corona and his sadness over Darkness that the precious artifact had completely slipped his mind.

Igneous's eyes went wide. "*You* have the shard?" he said. "Why didn't you tell us?"

"I forgot," Hunter explained. "I thought we were going to get killed, and then Corona almost died, and then Darkness..."

In the back of his mind, Hunter imagined Shadow's voice, chuckling. "You forgot!" the spider said. Hunter could almost see Shadow rolling his many eyes.

Lumen took the precious crystal from Hunter and gazed at it. "How did you obtain it?" he asked.

"Corona and I rescued it from the roach nest," Hunter explained.

"But I don't remember—" Corona began.

"You were kind of passed out at the time," Hunter said. "But I grabbed it before I dragged you out of the nest."

A broad smile broke over the prince's face. Princess Sparkle applauded.

"Well done, Hunter Steele!" Lumen said. "Your bravery is amazing! Your success, astonishing! To think that when none of my other riders could—"

Igneous interrupted. "Hunter Steele is *not* a Spider Rider, my prince," he said. "Not yet. He may have found a spider, but he has not passed the tests, and—"

"Who needs the tests?" Lumen blurted. "This is a time of crisis. Hunter has a spider, and he has done us invaluable service. I waive the tests." He gestured in the air, as if to make the traditional corps testing go away. "Right now," he concluded, "we need every available rider we have."

Igneous, Magma, and even Corona looked stunned.

"Does that mean I get to be a Spider Rider, too?" Princess Sparkle asked hopefully. "If you need every available rider—"

The prince cut her off. "Of course not," he said. "You're still too young. Besides, Father wouldn't approve."

"But I have a spider," Sparkle protested. "Hotarla is a very good spider!"

"She can barely carry your weight, Princess," Corona noted. "In time, you will take your place in the corps, but for now..."

"So why does Hunter get to be a rider and I don't?" the princess asked angrily. "Just because he rescued a shard—"

"I must say that I agree, my prince," Igneous put in. "Hunter is not ready to join the corps. His alliance with his spider is still uneasy, and he hasn't had the training."

"Then you must train him as you go," Lumen said. He looked sternly at the rest. "That's final. I have made my decision. Hunter Steele is to be outfitted with a manacle and given the proper weapons. See to it that he does well, Igneous."

Igneous bowed stiffly. "Yes, my prince."

Conflicting emotions warred within Hunter. He felt honored that the prince thought so highly of him. He felt proud to become a Spider Rider, even without passing the tests—whatever those might be. The idea of being bonded with a spider, though... Ugh! Darkness had been all right, for a spider, but Shadow... Well, Hunter didn't think he liked him. The huge black arachnid seemed entirely too arrogant.

"Oh, you'd know all about that," Shadow's voice said in Hunter's mind. "To tell you the truth, I'm not too keen on being bonded with you, either. If it hadn't been Darkness's last wish..."

"Quiet," Hunter said, not realizing that he spoke aloud as well as silently.

"Excuse me?" Corona asked.

"Nothing," Hunter replied. He smiled winningly at the Turandot girl.

She smiled back. "You must be very happy to be joining our ranks."

"Oh yes," Hunter said. "Very happy."

"Liar!" Shadow accused in his mind.

"Shut up!" Hunter thought back hard. Despite his feelings, he and Shadow were stuck together. Somehow, they'd have to work it out. "Ouch!" Someone had kicked Hunter in the shin.

Princess Sparkle looked up at him enviously. "Why do *you* get to be a rider?" she said. "I've been around longer. And my spider actually *likes* me."

"Does everyone know that Shadow and I don't get along?" Hunter wondered silently.

"Sparkle!" Lumen said. "Don't be a jealous pest. Everyone, follow me." He turned and walked to the far side of the room. A huge mosaic of a woman rider on spiderback covered the entire wall. Lumen quickly pressed a sequence of the brightly colored stones that made up the picture.

Silently, a crack formed in the wall, and a hidden door slid open. Lumen stepped inside, followed by Sparkle and the rest.

"Where are we going?" Hunter whispered to Corona.

"The Sacred Sepulcher," Corona whispered back, "where the Oracle resides—or did, until Mantid crippled her."

Hunter looked around at the solid stone passage they were descending into. The place looked as secure as a bank vault. "How did he manage that?" Hunter asked.

"No one is sure," Corona replied. "When it happened, a strange sleep overtook the city. It didn't last long enough for a full invasion. We suspect Mantid conducted a lightning raid into the chamber while we slept."

The passage wound deep into the heart of the plateau before opening out into a grand chamber with high ceilings. Blue-and-white polished marble formed the room's walls. The supports for the great vault looked like the legs of a giant spider holding up the sky.

In the center of the room stood a cracked golden statue of a beautiful woman. She had eight arms, as if she were a human spider. She wore Spider Rider armor and a long, flowing skirt. All but one of her arms were folded protectively over her chest. That one limb arced up, over her head, with its palm outstretched.

On her brow rested a spidery crown with eight hollows in it. The holes were arranged like the eyes of a spider. In one of the cavities blazed a red gemstone—twin to the one Hunter had recovered. All the rest of the depressions in the crown remained empty.

Prince Lumen approached the statue and pressed the new crystal into one of the openings. Slowly, one of the statue's arms lifted up, away from her body to match the one already above her head. A flickering red fire sprang up between the outstretched hands above the statue's head.

The ancient rider's eyes seemed to come alive with energy. One of the cracks in the statue's battered form mended itself.

Gradually, the features of the statue changed. The cold metal warmed to the color of human flesh.

The Oracle opened her eyes.

Hunter nearly jumped out of his skin.

"My children," the Oracle said. Her voice was pleasant and soft, though it filled the entire chamber. Hunter couldn't be sure if he was hearing her with his ears or his mind or both.

The other riders all bowed. Feeling awkward, Hunter did the same.

"I remain weak," the Oracle continued, "but some of my essence has been reborn. I sense that our city is in great peril, though I cannot see clearly enough to tell you why or how soon the catastrophe may befall us."

"Is it the Earthen's fault?" Sparkle blurted.

The Oracle smiled at the princess. "I cannot tell, my child," she said. "The future remains unclear. Once my shards are restored, I shall know better."

"Now that your voice is restored, can you tell us where to find the other shards?" Igneous asked.

The Oracle shook her head. "I cannot," she said. "My time grows short. Without the fragments from my crown, my powers remain severely depleted...." With that, her voice faded and her face returned to ordinary stone.

"A lot of good that did us," Magma said.

"Are you disrespecting the Oracle?" Igneous asked, anger flaring in his eyes.

"Don't worry, Igneous," Lumen said. "We already know the location of the third shard."

"We do?" Corona and Igneous asked simultaneously.

"Yes," Lumen said. "Petra discovered the information while you were gone. The shard is in the kingdom of the Snowmites. Mantid has apparently scattered the lost pieces throughout the world, hoping to keep them from us." The young prince drew himself up to a regal height. "His plan will fail."

"My troop will set out immediately, then," Igneous said. "Corona...Magma..."

"Lumen's already sent someone," Sparkle boasted.

Igneous arched one eyebrow. "Really? Who?"

"Since you were away on another task, I sent Petra and her legion," Lumen said.

"Was that wise, my prince?" Igneous asked. "Petra is a fine warrior, but she can be somewhat impulsive. Tactics are not her strong point."

The prince waved his hand dismissively. "I'm sure she'll do fine," he said. "She loves the kingdom as much as anyone."

Igneous slowly nodded and said, "Yes, my prince."

Prince Lumen smiled. "Your next task, Igneous, is to teach Hunter Steele everything he needs to know to be a great Spider Rider." He looked from Hunter to Igneous. "I'm assigning him to your squad."

Igneous nodded again. He didn't look too pleased.

In Hunter's mind, the sarcastic voice of Shadow echoed. "Terrific."

King Arachna frowned when informed of his son's choice to make an Earthen a Spider Rider.

"Ebony supports my decision," the prince told his father.

Something in Lumen's voice told Hunter that the prince hadn't been sure his father would approve. For a moment,

Hunter thought the king would reverse his son's decision. Slowly, though, Arachna XXIII nodded.

Prince Lumen smiled ever so slightly.

In the hours that followed, Hunter felt as though he had been swept into a whirlwind.

The riders took Hunter to the Forge, a grand marble building in the palace complex. Carvings of spiders ran up the walls from the steps to the topmost spire. Billows of white steam issued from a great chimney.

Inside, Hunter changed into a silken set of Spider rider clothing. He tried not to think about where the silk must have come from: spiders. Then Corona led him into a huge, windowless chamber.

The room stretched at least four stories high. There were seats arrayed around the room, but they were empty, perhaps due to the sudden nature of Hunter's initiation. Only Magma and the spiders of those present occupied the gallery. The spiders exchanged wary glances.

"They don't think you can do this," Shadow said in Hunter's mind. "I don't think you can do it, either."

"I *can*," Hunter thought back.

On one side of the chamber, beneath a titanic sculpture of a spider, stood two halves of a metal, cocoon-shaped pod.

King Arachna, Prince Lumen, and Princess Sparkle sat on a raised platform to the left of the pod. Igneous, arrayed in full battle armor, stood to the right.

Hunter glanced warily at the huge metal spider, whose eyes glowed slightly red. "Don't worry," Corona whispered in his ear. "Just do what you're told."

She led him to the platform, then stepped back. King Arachna and his children stood. Prince Lumen handed the king a jeweled box. The king opened it, revealing a silver spider-shaped bracelet. The king and prince looked gravely at Hunter. The princess tried to look serious, as well, but didn't quite succeed.

"This is your manacle," the king intoned. He took the bracelet from the box and wrapped it around Hunter's right wrist. "It binds you to our cause. You will wear it continuously during your time as a Spider Rider."

"May it gleam as brightly as your service to Arachnia," Lumen said.

"May it protect you as you protect the kingdom," Sparkle added solemnly.

"Swear the oath," the king commanded.

Corona took Hunter to Igneous, on the other side of the open pod.

Igneous looked at Hunter sternly. "Do you swear to uphold the code of the Spider Riders, to swear allegiance to Arachnia, to forsake all other goals until our nation's safety is assured?"

Hunter nodded. "I do," he said.

Igneous frowned at him. "You have to say 'I swear,'" he whispered.

"I swear," Hunter repeated.

"Oh, really?" Shadow echoed in his mind. "I thought you wanted to get home."

"Not now!" Hunter thought back.

Igneous glared at him, as though guessing the exchange between Hunter and the spider. "In the fire of the Forge," Igneous said, "may all doubts and deception be burned away."

Hunter looked up as two people, a man and a woman, clad

in heavy aprons carried pieces of insect armor into the room. They climbed up onto the back of the giant spider. Hunter now realized that the sculpture contained a huge cauldron.

As the man and woman fed the exoskeletons into the cauldron, the sculpture's eyes flared bright orange. Steam rose from the back of the titanic metal spider.

In the gallery, Shadow, Ebony, Venus, and the other spiders watching swayed in unison. A low thrumming sound filled the chamber.

"Enter the Forge," Igneous commanded. He pointed to an area between the two halves of the metal pod.

Hunter took a deep breath to summon his courage and stepped where Igneous indicated.

Immediately, the two halves of the pod clamped tight around Hunter. He looked up and saw that the top of the case remained open. The glowing eyes of the huge metal spider glared down at him from above.

The maw of the spider opened, and white-hot metal poured down into the pod. Fear clutched at Hunter's stomach as sparks, flame, and molten metal surrounded him. Everything became unbearably hot, though he did not die. The fires of the Forge blazed around him.

In his mind, he heard the droning of the spiders outside his metal prison. The heat became unbearable. He felt as though any moment his flesh would melt from his bones. He couldn't breathe. He screamed.

And then it ended.

The halves of the pod slid away. Hunter remained standing between the royal family and Igneous, head of the armies of Arachnia.

Gleaming, form-fitting metal covered his body—the diamond-hard armor of a Spider Rider.

The Turandot in the chamber, even Igneous, applauded.

Corona stepped close to him and smiled. "Now," she said, "you're one of us."

Igneous appeared on his other side. The older rider frowned. "Not yet," he said. "But he has taken the first step."

20
The Lost Legion

The next day Hunter Steele gazed at the power manacle on his wrist. It looked like a chunky silver bracelet, formed in the shape of a spider. The spider's legs encircled Hunter's arm and twined together so there was no way to take the manacle off. Hunter tried not to think about that too much.

"Arachna power!" he said, gripping the manacle in his opposite hand to activate the device as he'd been instructed.

The manacle glowed. Hunter's new Spider Rider armor flowed out of the bracelet and formed around his body. In seconds, he transformed from an ordinary human into a battle-ready Spider Rider. The metal trim on his armor gleamed. A shield with spider designs appeared, slung on his back, and a long lance grew in Hunter's armored hand.

"Cool!" Hunter thought.

"Not bad," Shadow thought back.

Organic armor had grown around the spider's chitinous skin, as well. He now looked something like a walking battle tank.

"Defend yourself!" Igneous said. He and Flame leaped across the giant, netlike web toward Hunter.

Hunter retrieved the shield from his back and brought it up barely in time. Igneous's lance slammed against the shield, almost knocking Hunter off Shadow's back. "Ouch!" Hunter cried.

Flame wheeled, so Igneous could come in for another pass.

"Shadow, go!" Hunter said.

"Go where?" Shadow countered.

Before Hunter could answer, Igneous and Flame slammed into them again. Shadow lost his footing on the giant web and fell to the testing arena floor. Hunter's hands slipped from the spider's reins. He toppled as well.

The spider landed lightly on his eight legs, but Hunter hit the ground hard. The air rushed out of Hunter's lungs in one big whoosh. His armor sizzled slightly where Igneous's lance had whacked it.

Igneous and Flame climbed off the net and stood over the defeated boy and spider. "You were lucky my lance and manacle were only set on training mode," Igneous said. "You have a lot to learn."

"Could I have a teacher who's less rough?" Hunter asked, rubbing his backside.

Igneous smiled unsympathetically. "We'll go again," he said. "Mount up, and climb to the web."

Hunter sighed and picked himself up off the floor.

Magma, standing by the side of the training area, laughed. "Many call this the school of hard knocks," he said.

"I've heard of that before," Hunter said. "But I thought it was just an expression."

"Not in Arachnia," Magma replied.

"Again!" Igneous commanded. "Defend yourself!" He raised his lance once more.

Just then, the door to the training room opened, and Prince Lumen walked in. Behind him came Corona and Sparkle.

As the prince stood in the center of the room, the riders present, including Hunter, bowed. Only Sparkle and Magma did not, though Magma dipped his head slightly. Lumen looked haughtily at the mercenary, then turned to the rest of the group.

"I have a new assignment for your legion, Igneous," the prince said. "An urgent mission."

"Yes, my prince?" Igneous replied.

"We have lost contact with Petra," Lumen said. "She and her riders were supposed to return from the Ice Caves of the Snowmites four sleeps ago. Nor have we received any word from her."

"That's not good," Shadow thought in Hunter's mind.

"We fear that she and her legion may have been lost in their quest for the third shard," Lumen continued.

"Corona and I will see to it," Igneous said. "Magma, too, if you so desire."

Lumen nodded. "Take the Earthen, as well," he said.

"But, my prince," Igneous said, "he can barely stay on his spider."

"That's not *my* fault," thought Shadow. Hunter glared at him.

"He will learn on the way, then," Lumen said. "His surface-world insights have proved useful in the past. Plus, you are one rider short for your patrol, even with Magma included."

"Unless you count me as two," Magma said confidently.

Igneous's face remained impassive. "Very well," he said. Then, turning to the others, he added, "Gather your equipment. I'll meet you at the south wall."

"I don't have much to pack," Hunter thought to Shadow. "Meet you by the castle gate."

Hunter went to his apartment within the Spider Rider compound. The room wasn't much, just a small cubicle, about ten feet by ten feet carved into a tabletop plateau within the castle. To reach his quarters, Hunter had to climb a precarious set of stairs, which wound up the outside of the building.

The room had a cot, a storage area curtained off to one side, and a trophy case on one wall. The case was actually a set of small niches carved into the stone, each just the right size for a life force medallion. Hunter's case was bare at the moment. He wondered how soon he'd earn his first medallion.

"Doesn't even know how to ride and already thinking about winning medallions!" Shadow thought in his mind.

"Hey!" Hunter shot back. "Some privacy, please!"

"I just thought you should know that you're running late," Shadow said. "Igneous has gone to the outside wall already. Stop daydreaming."

"Mind your own business!" Hunter said, trying hard to shut the spider out of his mind.

He gathered his few things, including a spider-shaped canteen and a backpack for food. He'd been told his Spider Rider armor would protect him from most conditions of heat and cold. This was good, as Hunter didn't think his surface clothes would keep him warm in the snow.

As he was about to leave, Corona appeared in the doorway, carrying a bundle of food provisions. "Hi," she said. "I knew you hadn't gotten your food supplies yet."

"Thanks," Hunter said.

"You're all charged up?"

"I think so," Hunter said. "The manacle can only be recharged at the Forge, right?"

"Correct," Corona replied. "So we must make do with

what power we have while on our mission. Use the energy wisely."

"I will," Hunter said. "But my head is still kind of swimming with all the information you guys crammed into me over the last day."

"I know," Corona said. "It's unusual to rush through the initiation this way, but these are unusual times. Come on. We don't want to be late." She tossed Hunter the provisions, and the two of them ran down to the castle gate.

They found Shadow and Venus there, mounted up, then met Igneous and Magma at the south wall.

Igneous eyed Hunter up and down. "Try not to freeze," the rider commander said. "And try not to fall off."

Hunter nodded.

"Good comeback," Shadow said in the boy's mind.

"Shut up!" Hunter thought back.

Igneous rode Flame up and over the wall. Corona, Magma, and Hunter followed. Hunter leaned forward and clung desperately to the hairs on Shadow's back as he sat behind the great spider's legs.

"If you'd put your boots into the *riding spiracles*, you could stand up, you know," Shadow said. He flexed some hidden muscles, and two stirrup-like shapes opened on his armored back. "Give it a try."

"M-maybe next time," Hunter thought back. It was taking all his concentration not to barf.

"The other spiders don't think you'll make it," Shadow said. "They think you aren't cut out to be a Spider Rider."

"Tell them to mind their own business," Hunter said, anger fast replacing his nausea. "And tell them I *never* give up."

They quickly reached the ground and began galloping south, away from the city, along the edge of the mountains. Forest mixed with rolling plains ahead of them. While the course Igneous chose wasn't exactly flat, Hunter decided to try to learn a proper spider battle stance.

Cautiously, he got to his knees and then tried to stand. His snowboarding experience helped him. "I'll try those spiracles now," he thought to Shadow.

The spider obligingly opened the specialized breathing vents along his back. Hunter wedged his boot toes into them, as though he were sticking his feet into water skis. The orifices closed tightly around his toes, but he still wobbled a little.

"Just relax," Shadow said. "I won't let you fall."

"I wasn't worried," Hunter replied, trying not to.

"Well, not on purpose, anyway," Shadow added.

The spiders moved at great speed. Hunter judged that they galloped about as fast as a car drove on a highway. Still, the Ice Caves of the Snowmites lay a long way from Arachnia.

When they stopped to sleep, Corona drew Hunter a rough map in the sand. The spine of mountains on which the city rested ran far to the south. Beyond that were fields of snow, and beyond them lay the mountains that held the Snowmite caves.

Before sleeping, Igneous spent some time jousting with Hunter. Hunter got knocked off twice but counted it a victory when he stayed standing the third time. Igneous nodded appreciatively, which made Hunter feel good.

"We'll joust every spare moment we have," Igneous said to him. "Maybe by the time we reach the Ice Caves you'll know enough not to get killed."

Hunter rubbed his sore muscles and nodded. He slept like a rock, despite the ever-blazing eye of the Inner World sun staring down on them. Morning came too soon. Hunter's body still ached from the previous day's ride and training.

He didn't complain, and instead mounted up and rode with the rest. The telepathic bond he shared with Shadow told Hunter that the spider ached as well. The big black arachnid was far too proud to mention it, though.

After lunch, Hunter rode by sitting rather than standing. His legs just hurt too much to ride as the others did.

"I don't care what the other spiders think," Hunter told Shadow.

"I wasn't even going to mention it," Shadow thought back.

On the journey after the third sleep, the weather turned cold. Frost covered the tall brown grass and the bare limbs of the trees.

The trees grew smaller, then disappeared as the southern mountains rose into view. The sun dipped ever lower in the northern sky as they drew farther away from the core. Gray clouds rolled in overhead.

As the weather changed, Hunter's armor adjusted. Tiny heating elements came on inside, keeping him warm.

The land around them became fields of crusty snow. Low-hanging storm clouds blotted out the sun. Flurries dappled the air.

"Look," Magma said, pointing to some tracks on the icy ground.

Igneous nodded. "Petra's legion. The tracks go to the mountains, but they don't return. Concentrate, all of you. Perhaps we can reach their spiders with mind talk."

The whole group stopped and did as Igneous ordered.

"Nothing," said Magma, a few moments later.

"Nor with us," Corona added.

A chill ran down Hunter's spine. "Maybe they're—"

"Don't think that!" Shadow blurted in his mind. "Focus on the mission."

"Perhaps they're imprisoned," Igneous said. "We'll try again when we get closer."

They soon reached the mountain lair of the Snowmites.

"There's the opening, overhead," Magma said, pointing to a gaping cave mouth halfway up the mountain face.

"Petra went this way," Corona said, indicating a winding path up the mountainside. "Again, there's no indication any of the legion came out."

Hunter shivered. "Let's hope we don't become part of the lost legion, too," he said quietly.

"Don't think so loud," Shadow put in. "I don't need to hear that kind of stuff, and the other spiders certainly don't, either."

"Let's go," Igneous said. He and the rest began trooping up the narrow trail.

The going was difficult and treacherous. The ledge was barely large enough for one spider, and it constantly switched back on itself. Soon, though, an even smaller path broke off from the main trail.

"It looks like this new path leads straight to the cave opening," Magma said.

"It's too slick and narrow for the spiders," Corona countered. "The legion's tracks keep going uphill."

Igneous squinted into the blowing snow toward an opening in front of the ledge. "It looks as though Petra's troop may have dropped down from above."

"That would make sense," Magma said. "But it will take much longer to enter the lair that way."

"I agree," Igneous said. "That's why we'll go in on foot."

"What about the spiders?" Hunter asked.

"That's what we want to know, too," Shadow put in.

"Corona will take the spiders to the upper trail," Igneous said. Then, directly to her, he added, "Come as quickly as you can. We don't know what may await us on the other side of the cave entrance."

"Hunter," Shadow said urgently, "I feel something... something about the spiders with Petra. I think they're alive, but I can't really communicate with them."

Hunter relayed this information to the other riders.

"Brutus isn't getting any of that," Magma said.

"Nor Venus," Corona added.

Igneous looked at Hunter and his spider. "Flame is picking up something, too," he said. "Darkness was very strong in mind talk. It makes sense that his pupil would have a similar gift."

"I bet that's how Darkness was able to communicate with me so easily," Hunter thought.

"Naturally," Shadow agreed.

"All right," Corona said. "You three get going. I'll take the spiders and rappel down as quickly as we can. Good luck."

Hunter, Igneous, and Magma got off their spiders and headed for the entrance. Each of them activated his power manacle, and their rider armor flowed over them. The three armored humans moved carefully along the ledge toward the cave.

The entrance to the lair of the Snowmites looked like a huge open mouth with gigantic icicles for teeth. A deep shelf, much wider than the trail, spread out in front of it.

"How do the Snowmites get in and out?" Hunter asked as they approached. The area above and below the cave was sheer ice, and the narrow trail didn't seem a practical way for a whole population to move.

"Snowmites climb ice as easily as spiders climb walls," Magma said. "So, watch yourself in their lair. They could be coming at you from above, below, or either side."

"Terrific," Hunter said, meaning the opposite.

"Courage," Shadow said in his mind. The spider's voice seemed more faint and distant. Shadow may have had a gift for mind talk, but Hunter clearly hadn't mastered it yet.

The three riders reached the entrance shelf without incident. Magma peered cautiously around the corner of the cave.

"Magma says no guards," Shadow said in Hunter's mind. The spider's voice was almost a whisper now.

"I can hardly hear you," Hunter thought hard.

"You need...more training," Shadow replied faintly. "Igneous says to follow him in."

Hunter nodded to Igneous, and the patrol commander led them into the lair.

The entryway stretched like a frozen corridor into the mountainside. Icy stalactites hung from the passage ceiling; icy stalagmites jutted up from the floor.

The three Spider Riders wound cautiously through the obstacles, following the tracks of Petra's lost legion. The passage branched twice. Each time, they followed the spider tracks. They saw no sign of the Snowmites.

"I've lost Brutus," Magma said when they came to the third cross passage.

"I don't hear Shadow, either," Hunter said.

Igneous kept following the tracks. Ahead, the passage widened into a huge cavern. "I can still hear Flame...barely," Igneous said. "He says that Shadow claims we're getting close to the other spiders."

"Very close, it looks like," Magma said. He'd stopped dead at the entrance to the new cave.

The cavern ahead was enormous, stretching four stories high and reaching away from them for almost a city block. Clear blue-white ice formed the walls, the floor, and the ceiling of the cavern. The whole thing looked like a crystal throne room. It was unearthly, eerie, and beautiful.

It wasn't the cave's beauty that had caught Magma's attention, though.

On the far side of the cavern, below a crystalline balcony, stood a transparent wall.

The lost legion, four riders and their four spiders, stood embedded in the wall—frozen deep within the ice.

21
The Snowmites' Trap

Dungobeet found Mantid on a balcony high atop the Insector leader's enormous hive complex. The smaller bug and his circling messengers approached the master cautiously. Disturbing Mantid while he was thinking could be a fatal mistake. Mantid gazed covetously over his wide kingdom.

Dungobeet cleared his throat, making a sound something like a hoarse cricket.

Mantid turned just slightly. His huge cold eyes focused on his servant.

Dungobeet immediately began to quake nervously.

"Have you done as I've asked?" said Mantid.

"Yes, master," Dungobeet replied. "Everything is in place. Centok's army is on the move, as you have directed.

"And the Spider Riders?"

"The Snowmites assure me that they will be permanently... *delayed*."

Mantid formed his clawlike fingers into the shape of an arch. He looked pleased. "Good," he said. "Report to me when the city has fallen."

Dungobeet bowed again. "Yes, master."

Hunter gasped. A chill shot through his heart, as though he were trapped in ice, alongside the missing Spider Riders.

Igneous and Magma stood dumbfounded as well.

"They're still alive inside the ice," Igneous finally said. "That's what Shadow sensed."

"How can they be alive?" Hunter asked. "They're frozen!"

"You have much to learn, Earthen," Magma replied dismissively.

"Turandot spiders go into hibernation when it gets very cold," Igneous explained. "This would protect them from dying in the ice. As to the riders, their armor will keep them alive by providing air and warmth—until the power of their manacles is depleted."

Hunter glanced down at the silver bracelet on his own wrist. The red crystal set into it gleamed brightly, as it had since he'd donned it in the Forge.

He looked to Petra's legion, frozen in the ice wall at the back of the cavern. The crystals in their manacles still blinked, but very faintly. "They can't last much longer," Hunter said. "How can we get them out?"

Magma shook his head. "My plasma burst might break the ice, but it could harm the legion as well."

"My manacle's heat powers could melt them out," Igneous said, "given enough time." He looked around suspiciously. "But I'm not sure how much time we have."

Magma nodded. "I'm surprised the Snowmites haven't attacked us yet. They must be planning some kind of trap. We should get out of here quickly. What initial power did the Forge give your manacle, Earthen?"

"Sonic charge," Hunter replied. "But I haven't used it yet." He grinned sheepishly. "Too busy training."

Igneous frowned. "That would break the ice, but the noise would surely bring the Snowmites."

"Maybe we can chip them out with our swords or lances,"

Hunter suggested. "If you used your heat powers to melt the ice at the same time..."

"That might work," Igneous agreed. "It's worth a try, anyway." He and Hunter stepped into the cavern and headed toward the lost legion. Magma followed.

The cavern floor sloped down, forming a slight bowl. Though stalactites hung from the ceiling, the floor of the cave remained as smooth as an ice rink. The riders slipped and slid a bit as they crossed toward their frozen comrades.

Magma sniffed the air. "Does it seem a bit warm and humid here to anyone else, or is it just me?" he asked.

He looked up. His sharp eyes scanned the chamber and settled on the ice ledge above the frozen legion. "Mites!" he hissed.

Hunter and Igneous looked up as a dozen Snowmites, horrible, white-carapaced creatures with mouths like pincers, moved a huge iron cauldron toward the edge of the precipice. Wisps of steam rose from the cauldron.

In an instant, Hunter realized what was happening. The Snowmites were going to pour water down on him and the others—just as they had done to Petra's legion. The water would freeze almost instantly, trapping them inside forever.

Igneous and Magma brought up their manacles. "Hunter!" Igneous commanded.

Hunter raised his braceleted arm as well.

"Plasma burst!" Magma said. An energy blast streaked from his fist and smashed into the Snowmites carrying the cauldron. The mites scattered, blown away from the blast. They dropped the cauldron, and it tipped forward. Water began to pour down the icy cliff.

"Now, Earthen!" Igneous commanded.

"Sonic charge!" Hunter called, activating his manacle's power.

A sudden, deafening burst of noise filled the room. Fortunately, his armor's automatic systems kicked in to protect his ears, so he caught only the slightest bit of it. Still, the noise made his head ring.

The sonic charge blasted out in all directions, shattering the ice wall in front of them and shaking the chamber to its core. Millions of tiny ice fragments filled the room. Several stalactites crashed down from above.

The Snowmites shrieked and covered their earholes but managed to tip the cauldron all the way over.

Igneous pointed his manacle at the falling water. "Heat ram!" he commanded.

Waves of blistering heat shot out from his manacle, immediately turning the falling water into steam.

The Snowmites wailed and fled from the cavern as the hot mist hit them.

Magma dusted the fallen ice crystals off his armor. "Well, that was impressive," he said, looking at Hunter. After Hunter's sonic charge, the three riders' ear protectors had retracted once more.

"Impressive yes," Igneous agreed, "but I'm sure it alerted the entire hive as well. Next time, try to control your power better."

"Sorry," Hunter said. "Like I told you, this was my first time using it."

Already the sounds of angry Snowmites buzzing through the hive echoed all around them. Without the ice wall blocking their way, the riders now saw a dozen entrances into the room, besides the one they'd come in. There were at least two openings on the ledge above as well, though getting up to them without a spider to climb the walls would be difficult.

"What now?" Hunter asked.

"Now we find the shard," Igneous said, "before the mites find us."

"That'll be tricky," said a tired-sounding female voice. "The Snowmites are everywhere."

Petra and three other Spider Riders emerged from the ruins of the ice wall with their spiders. Hunter's heart soared. He'd been so startled by the effects of his sonic charge, that he'd momentarily forgotten about the lost legion. Apparently, his thundering sonic blast had freed them all!

Petra was a slender young woman about Igneous's age, with short dark hair and piercing green eyes. Green striping covered her spider's black armor. There were two young men and one other girl in her legion. All four looked tired and stiff, as did their spiders. But they seemed little the worse for wear otherwise.

"Did you explore any of the tunnels?" Igneous asked Petra.

"No," she replied. "We were ambushed immediately when we entered. I'm glad you found us."

Igneous nodded and smiled. "Thank the new boy for freeing you so quickly," he said.

Petra gave Hunter a curt nod. Hunter tried not to blush.

"Where are your spiders?" Petra asked Igneous.

"Corona is bringing them," Igneous said. "We left them behind and crossed the narrow ledge to search more quickly."

"That's almost foolhardy for you, Igneous," Petra said with a sly grin. "Let's hope it's not a fatal mistake."

"Discussion later," Magma said. "Right now we need to find the shard and get out of here."

"I'm with Magma," Hunter said. The sounds of approaching Snowmites were building in the cave like distant thunder.

Petra looked to Igneous. "What's the plan?"

Suddenly, Snowmites swarmed into the cavern from all sides. They crawled across the ceilings and walls and scampered over the floors. The slick, icy surface didn't slow them down at all.

"The plan," Igneous said, "is to stay alive long enough to figure out our next move."

With that, he powered up his lance and charged into the nearest group of mites.

22
The Third Shard

Hunter dodged as a Snowmite leaped at him from the ceiling. He drew his stun sword, and manacle power surged through the weapon. When the mite rose and attacked again, he swung at its head. He smashed the flat of the blade against the back of the mite's neck, and the Snowmite went sprawling.

Igneous and Magma attacked with their lances, and the mites trying to get them fell quickly.

Petra and her riders sprang into action. Though their movements seemed slow and somewhat clumsy compared to the Spider Riders who hadn't been frozen, they were still dervishes of action. "Conserve manacle energy!" Petra ordered. "Unpowered weapons only!"

Hunter thought she must have been cautioning everyone, because if she only meant her legion, she could have just mind-talked the information to them.

"Petra," Igneous said as he knocked down three mites with his lance, "protect our backs while we search for the shard."

Petra nodded and Igneous ran toward one of the nearby mite-clogged entryways. "Magma!" he called.

"C'mon, Earthen," Magma said, following their group commander's lead. He fired a plasma burst over their heads and into a swarm of oncoming mites. The mites scattered as though they were tenpins hit by a bowling ball. The three

Spider Riders skidded past their downed foes and entered the tunnel beyond.

"Why this tunnel?" Hunter asked as they went.

"It had the fewest mites in it," Igneous explained.

"Now all our troubles are behind us," Magma added with a wry smile.

They ran quickly down the passageways, seemingly guided by an inner sense possessed by Igneous alone. They would pass one tunnel, then take another, then turn into a third, then skip a fourth.

"Does he know where he's going?" Hunter whispered to Magma after they'd been running for five minutes.

"He's heading deeper into the mountain," Magma explained. "The mites would have the shard well hidden."

"I'm also looking for tracks," Igneous added. "The passage we want will have had regular traffic but not too much. Guard mites only, probably. I'm looking for the distinctive markings of their feet."

"That's why he's Prince Lumen's chief commander," Magma said. He winked at Hunter. "I think those are the marks you're looking for," the mercenary said, pointing to a small passageway.

Igneous pulled up short. "Always right, are you, sword-for-hire?" he asked.

"Most of the time," Magma replied.

He motioned to the new passage, and all three of them crawled inside. Hunter wondered if the tunnel was so small to make it easier to defend. He also wondered what kind of traps or guards they might find waiting for them at the other end.

"We're in luck," Igneous said from the front of the line. "The fighting in the entryway seems to have drawn away the guards." He stepped out into the small cavern beyond. Magma and Hunter followed him.

Before them stood a cylinder of ice, ten feet thick. Floating in the middle was the third shard of the Oracle.

"How long would it take to melt it out?" Magma asked.

"Too long," Igneous replied. "Hunter, use your sonic charge."

Hunter nodded and activated the weapon. This time, his armor protected his ears before the first blaring sound. The ice cylinder flew to pieces. Hunter wondered if his armor had learned to avoid the sound or if he had subconsciously commanded it to shield his ears.

Igneous stooped and picked up the red, gemlike shard. "They'll be coming now," he said. "Let's go."

The sonic boom had cracked the walls of the chamber as well as destroyed the shard's crystalline prison. However, it hadn't done enough damage to enlarge the crawlway through which they'd entered.

Hunter and the others squeezed through as quickly as they could. But when they reached the far end, they found the corridor swarming with Snowmite warriors.

Hunter activated his sonic charge again. The passage shook, and the Snowmites fell back, reeling.

Igneous picked the weakest part of the Insectors' line and led the three of them through it, knocking down the stunned mites as they went. Hunter's armor hummed oddly. He looked down and saw the crystal on his manacle flashing, growing dimmer. He'd used up a lot of power with the blasts.

The mites closed in around them. Igneous and Magma used their manacle powers to drive the Insectors back. Their manacles began to flash as well, though not as badly as Hunter's. Clearly, they knew how to use their powers more effectively than he did.

"Keep fighting!" Igneous ordered.

Hunter swatted at the mites with his sword. He wished he'd had more time to practice before going out on this mission. He wished he hadn't used so much power on each of his sonic charges. He wished, for the first time, that Shadow were here to help him.

They rounded an icy corner with the mites hot on their trail. As they did, they nearly crashed into the lost legion. Petra's Spider Riders looked even more battered and weary than they had before.

"What are you doing?" Igneous asked.

"Coming to save you," Petra replied. "Our spiders got worried."

The look on Igneous's face said he thought this an unlikely story. "What about the exit?" he asked.

"Clear, all the way back," Petra responded. "We've decoyed them away from it."

"What are we waiting for, then?" Magma said. "Let's get out of here!"

Petra's people pulled Hunter and the rest aboard their spiders, and they all scuttled back toward the cliff face entrance. As they reached the main cavern, the mites caught up. The pale Insectors swarmed in from all directions.

The riders kept going, pausing only long enough to bash a few mite warriors out of their way.

"HIZZ-AHHH!" Magma cried as he clouted one on the head with his lance. "Too bad we don't have time to stop to collect a few life force medallions."

"Consider yourself lucky they're not collecting those of our spiders, instead," Petra replied.

"Yes," Magma replied, shooting her a smile, "good thing you got frozen rather than captured and dispatched."

Petra gave him a cold stare in return.

They reached the entrance quickly. The mites had all massed behind them for the chase, rather than trying to cut them off.

"We're lucky their leaders aren't smarter," Igneous noted.

"Mantid's pretty clever," Petra said. "Good thing he's not here." She looked around the ledge at the cave entrance. "Web shreds!" she cursed.

"What's wrong?" Magma asked.

"The web lines we used to climb down from above," she said. "They're gone! There are no solid rocks here, only ice. Without the lines, we're trapped here on the cliff face!"

Princess Sparkle dashed into the throne room, sweat streaming down her young brow.

"Sparkle," her father said, "have you and Hotarla been out after curfew again?" Prince Lumen, standing next to the king, frowned at his sister.

"Yes, Father," Sparkle replied. "But—"

"No buts, young lady," the king said. "You're not a Spider Rider yet—even though you may think you are."

"But, Father—"

"If this happens again, I'll have to separate you from Hotarla," the king said.

"But, Dad, we saw a huge army of Centipedians heading this way!" the princess blurted.

Both the king and Prince Lumen paled.

"Can this be true?" the king asked his son.

Lumen shook his head and frowned. "Sparkle," he said, "where did you see these Insectors?"

"Less than a sleep away," Sparkle replied, "as a 'pede scuttles. They're hiding in the forest and creeping this way. They're swinging around the town they ruined last time to avoid our sentries."

"Bursting a dam won't save us this time," the king said gravely. He headed for an ordinary suit of armor hanging on the wall nearby. "I'll go find out if what she says is true."

"Of course it's true!" Sparkle protested.

"Father, wait," Lumen said. "I can handle this. It's my job after all." He concentrated a moment. "Ebony and I are sending out scouts to discover the enemy's exact position. We're also sending militia runners to warn the towns in their path, so they'll be ready."

"What about the legions that went to the Ice Caves?" Sparkle asked. "Shouldn't we warn them, ask them to come back to the city right away?"

"They aren't responding," the king said. "Something must be wrong."

"Could this be the catastrophe the Oracle warned of?" Lumen wondered aloud. He shook his fist in frustration. "With so many riders abroad, we're severely depleted."

"I could go south to find them," Sparkle offered.

"I forbid it," the king and Lumen said simultaneously.

"You are not to leave the castle," the king finished.

Princess Sparkle pouted. "But—"

"No buts, young lady," the king warned. "Just do as I say."

Sparkle nodded. But in her mind, she was already plotting her route out of the city and to the caves of the Snowmites.

23
Shadow from Above

Hunter glanced toward the cave entrance behind the Turandot warriors. The sound of the rampaging mites heading their way built like thunder. He pictured the Insectors catching them and encasing them all in a block of ice until their manacle power ran out and they died.

Or worse, he imagined the mites overwhelming them and pushing them over the edge of the cliff. The spiders and their riders might be tough, but Hunter doubted that any of them could survive a thousand-foot fall.

"I could make web chutes," said one of Petra's legion, a short, curly-haired teen. "But it'll take time."

"We don't *have* any time," Magma said.

"Save yourself, Geode," Igneous commanded. "Take the shard with you and go. Return to Arachnia."

The teenage boy looked at the riders' leader, a mixture of sadness and admiration in his eyes. "I don't know if the chute will hold up in these winds," he said. "It could be a lost cause. Maybe, if I stay, we can fight our way out of this."

Igneous shook his head. "The rest of us will hold off the mites as long as we can." He handed the shard to Geode, then turned and walked back into the cave entrance to make a final stand.

"Good luck, Geode," the others said as they went to help Igneous.

Only Hunter remained behind, unable to find either his voice or his courage.

Geode and his spider began weaving a parachute-like web atop the cliff.

Hunter forced himself to the cave entrance, to stand beside the rest. This was a terrible way for his first mission as a Spider Rider to end, but it was better than dying like a coward.

The mites surged toward them in droves. The tired riders and their spiders prepared to fight.

"Save your manacle energy," Igneous cautioned. "Use it only as a last resort."

Hunter and the others nodded their understanding.

The mites crashed against the riders like an icy wave. The bugs swarmed over the walls and ceiling as well as the floor. Petra's remaining spiders leaped high into the air, keeping the mites on the ceiling from bypassing them and dropping down onto the spiderless riders.

Igneous and Magma used their lances furiously, batting mites off the walls. Hunter swung his sword at those who made it past the others. He was the last line of defense between the mites and Geode.

Hunter set his jaw, determined not to let any Insector get through. Two mites fell easily before him.

A third parried Hunter's sword with its own spear, then clouted the boy in the side on the backswing. The blow clanked off Hunter's armor, but it staggered him.

The mite pressed forward. Hunter backed up, trying to get

under the Insector's guard. The Snowmite thrust its spear between Hunter's ankles, tripping him.

Hunter fell onto the icy ledge. As the mite tried to get past him, Geode and his spider rocketed forward.

"Geode, no!" Hunter cried as the young rider smashed into the Snowmite. For a moment, an image of utter failure flashed through Hunter's mind. He saw the mites capturing not only the riders, but the shard as well. Arachnia would be left practically defenseless, lacking not only its Oracle, but also some of its best Spider Riders.

A shadow fell over Hunter, and his heart froze. Had the mites forged ahead so quickly after he'd fallen?

"What are you so worried about?" asked a familiar voice in his head.

"Shadow!" Hunter cried, overjoyed.

He looked up as Corona, Venus, Shadow, and the other spiders rappelled down the cliff face on web lines. Corona winked at him as she and Venus slid to ground level.

The reinforcements charged the Snowmites massed at the cave entrance. Igneous and Magma quickly swung onto their spiders' backs. It took Hunter a moment longer to mount up, but soon he joined the fray as well.

"Boy, am I glad to see you!" Hunter thought to Shadow.

"Don't get mushy, Earthen," Shadow mind-talked back.

Hunter ignored the spider's sarcasm and used his lance to help drive the mites back into the cavern. He wasn't very skilled yet, but he and the other riders formed a powerful unit.

"Webs!" Igneous cried as the mites fell back.

Simultaneously, all the spiders began casting webs across the tunnel entrance. The gooey masses didn't stick very well to the ice, but they did slow the retreating mites.

Corona pointed her gauntlet at the cliff face above the cave. "Lightning lance!" she cried.

White energy blazed from her manacled hand and blasted into the cliff face. It collapsed in a huge heap of rubble, covering the webbed-up entrance. "That should hold them for a while," she said.

Igneous examined the rubble. "There's enough stone here to anchor to," he said.

"Anchor for what?" Hunter wondered silently.

"We're going to rappel down the cliff face," Shadow said, "the same way we arrived from above. This is a much bigger drop, though."

Hunter's stomach clenched a bit at the thought, but he maintained a brave face.

"Don't worry," Shadow said. "I won't let you fall."

"Not even accidentally," Hunter warned him.

The spider laughed in his mind. "You're no fun!"

The Spider Riders made some quick preparations, then headed down the cliff face before the mites could dig free.

They stopped to reanchor their web lines on several rocky outcroppings along the way. The trip down was dizzying for Hunter, but he managed to hang onto the hairs on Shadow's back. True to his word, the spider did not let Hunter fall.

Once they reached the cliff bottom, Geode returned the shard to Igneous. "As group leader, you should have this," he said.

Igneous nodded and took the crystal. He gave the command to move out, and all of them headed north, back toward the distant city. Hunter thought Petra looked slightly jealous of their commander.

"The two of them have something of a rivalry," Shadow said in Hunter's head.

"Would you stop doing that!" Hunter thought.

"Stop doing what?" Shadow asked.

"Stop popping into my head out of the blue all the time," Hunter said. "Don't you ever knock?"

"That's a silly question," Shadow remarked. "What do you expect me to knock on, your skull?"

"You know what I mean."

"I'll try not to startle you so much," the spider replied. "As I was saying, Petra and Igneous have a bit of a rivalry. They attended the academy together and were always jousting to be lead in their class. But Igneous is Lumen's favorite, so..."

"Why?" Hunter asked. "Why is Igneous Lumen's favorite?"

"Well, two main reasons, as near as the other spiders tell me," Shadow said. "One is that he and Lumen have been friends practically since Lumen was born. The second is that—no matter what Petra may think—Igneous really is the best rider in the kingdom."

"Better than Magma?" Hunter asked.

"Magma isn't part of the corps," Shadow explained. "So he kind of doesn't count. But even then, Igneous is the best tactician the Turandot have."

"Not so much chatter," Igneous said aloud.

"He can hear us?" Hunter thought.

"Not really," Shadow replied. "Not unless I want him to. But the other spiders can hear us speaking, the same way you know two people are talking in a crowded room, even if you can't make out the words."

The group rode out of the ice fields before stopping to rest. All of them felt exhausted from their ordeal. The riders' manacles were almost depleted as well, all save Corona's since she'd missed most of the fighting.

Because the weapons could be recharged only in the Forge, Igneous hoped they could make it back to Arachnia without further incident.

"The Snowmites won't leave their icy kingdom," Petra assured him, "not even to follow the shard."

"That doesn't mean they might not contact other Insectors, though," Magma reminded her. "Some of their kind can fly. Unfortunately, we can't."

They made camp at the edge of a small stand of trees on the grassy plains. The spiders spun webs between the trunks to ward off intruders, and Igneous set watches. Hunter, being the least experienced, was assigned to watch last.

"That way, you'll be fully rested and alert," Igneous said.

"If I can even get to sleep in the first place," Hunter thought. He'd come close to dying today—too close to rest easily.

He did sleep, though nightmares plagued him. First he dreamed that he was caught between a freezing river and a boiling pit. Snowmites surrounded him, trying to force Hunter to fall off a narrow ice bridge.

Something grabbed him, not a mite, but a huge spider, intent on sucking his blood out. Hunter tried to scream, but sticky webs covered his mouth.

"Wake up!" someone said to him.

He struggled, but the monster held him tight.

"Wake up," said another voice, Corona's this time.

Hunter woke up to see her standing next to him. She looked concerned.

"What's wrong?" he asked. He felt slightly surprised that it wasn't night outside. Then he remembered the Inner World had no nights.

"It's your watch," she said.

He nodded sleepily.

"I'll sit up with you for a bit," Corona said.

"Because I'm inexperienced?" Hunter asked. He felt embarrassed at having to be helped all the time.

"No," she said, "because I...I feel that something's not quite right."

"Okay," Hunter said. He felt slightly relieved not to be sitting guard on his own. He and Corona took their places, sitting easily on the backs of their spiders.

"Don't worry, boy," Shadow thought in his mind. "You and the girl can chat. Venus and I will handle most of the watching."

"Chat about what?" Hunter asked. The spider didn't reply.

Suddenly, Corona stood. She looked anxiously toward the plains beyond the trees. Something was moving through the tall, thick grass surrounding the tiny forest.

"Yes, Venus," she said aloud. "I hear it."

"Venus is waking the others," Shadow informed Hunter.

"What?" Hunter said. "Why?"

Suddenly, the grass before them parted and out rambled a very tired-looking spider and rider. The girl was covered nearly head to foot in dirt and grime, and so was her spider. Hunter almost didn't recognize them.

"Sparkle," Igneous said angrily, "what are you doing out here? You should be at the castle." The riders' leader rubbed the sleep from his eyes.

"Lumen and father said I was too young to help, but we did a good job, didn't we, Hotarla?" She patted her spider proudly.

"Good job at what, princess?" Petra asked. "What are you talking about?"

"Someone had to warn you," Sparkle said, "and Lumen couldn't spare anyone else. So Hotarla and I came."

"Warn us about what?" Magma asked sternly.

"The Centipedians are coming," she said. "Arachnia city is under attack!"

"What news from your spies?" Mantid asked Dungobeet.

"They fly with hurricane speed to bring you news from the battlefront," Dungobeet said. He bowed slightly.

Mantid said nothing. The beetlelike Insector bowed again, then continued. "Prince Lumen rides out to meet Centok's force," Dungobeet said. "He is bringing all his Spider Riders."

"Those not currently trapped in our ice caves," Mantid said. A wicked smile creased his armored face. "It will not be enough to save the city."

"No, your greatness," Dungobeet said. "Not nearly enough. They show no signs of having guessed your brilliant plan."

Satisfied, Mantid folded his clawlike fingers on his lap. "Good," he said. "Before the humans realize what is happening, Centok will breach the city walls. The defenses of

Arachnia will crumble. Then the reign of humanity will end in this Inner World."

Dungobeet smiled. "The city will fall," he said gleefully. "Then the era of Mantid will begin!"

24
City Under Siege

"The 'pede army is huge," Sparkle said breathlessly. "Even bigger than the one at the dam burster battle."

"Centok must be making an all-out attack," Igneous said, "trying to destroy the city while it's weakened."

"With all of us here and the Oracle out of commission," Petra said, "the kingdom is at a real disadvantage."

"The Insectors are using the jungles as cover," Sparkle continued. "There are thousands of them—maybe hundreds of thousands. And they're bringing weapons I've never seen before, too."

"More of Mantid's tricks, no doubt," Corona said.

"Only the Oracle can save Arachnia now," Geode said.

"The Oracle...and the bravery of the Spider Riders," Magma added.

Hunter nodded grimly.

Shadow's voice echoed in Hunter's mind. "Well, kid, this is it," the spider said, "all-out war with the Insectors. Do you think you can handle it?"

"I already told you," Hunter replied. "I *never* give up. I swore I was with the riders until the end."

"So, does that mean you're ready?"

"More than ready," Hunter replied.

In his mind, he felt the spider smile.

"Mount up," Igneous commanded. "We ride like the wind for Arachnia!"

Prince Lumen smashed another 'pede with his lance and looked around. He and his riders had felled hundreds of Insectors, but thousands more surged forward to take their place.

The Spider Riders' battle to keep the enemy far from Arachnia had failed. Even now, Lumen's forces were being pressed back toward the cliff face at the bottom of the city.

Huge catapults fired from the back of the Insector lines, hurling balls of burning pitch into the midst of the defenders. The Turandot spiders ducked nimbly out of the way, but the constant fire made it hard to form a cohesive line of defense.

Even as the riders tried to rally, the bugs fired their weapons over the walls and into the city. The sound of alarm bells blared within Arachnia as firefighters ran to quench the new blazes.

The prince felt confident that the city volunteers could control the fires set by the enemy. His heart ached. Such destruction had never come to Arachnia before! Even as he fought the Insectors with all his might, he wished he could do more.

The prince's eyes scanned the battlefield. The red-armored centipede commander lurked near the back lines of the fight. He moved among the Centipedians, directing the aim of their fiery catapults.

"If I could take Centok out," Lumen thought, "the morale of the Centipedians might break."

"A bold move," Ebony, the prince's battle spider, agreed.

"The Insectors will never expect it. We'll leap over the 'pedes separating us and take him by surprise."

Lumen nodded grimly. "Inform the other Spider Riders of our plan," he commanded Ebony. "Tell them to hold the Insector army, at all costs, until we return."

Ebony surged forward, his powerful legs leaping over the Insectors battling before them. The Centipedians looked up as the prince of the Spider Riders passed. They stabbed at Lumen and his mount, but their spears bounced off the arachnid's armor.

The startled bugs fell back as the princely rider leaped forward.

"They're frightened of us!" Lumen thought with satisfaction.

"They should be," Ebony said in his mind.

Four more huge leaps took Prince Lumen deep into the Centipedian troops. The bug commander turned, startled to see the rider among them. He commanded the catapults to fire at the prince.

Lumen and Ebony were too quick.

They landed amid the bug commander's bodyguards. Eight armored legs and a manacle-powered lance flashed out. Ten guards fell, clearing the way to Centok himself.

The Centipedian leader seemed frozen in terror.

Ebony jumped forward. Prince Lumen aimed his lance at the black scorpion carrying the bug commander. The scorpion's tail flashed forward, trying to sting the prince and his mount.

Lumen batted the creature's tail aside and hit the vulnerable spot below its jaw. The scorpion collapsed, pitching Centok forward. The Centipedian leader hit the ground, next to his downed steed.

Prince Lumen leaped from Ebony's back as Centok tried to rise. The Spider Rider leader landed on the ground next to the villain. He put his armored foot on Centok's chest.

The Centipedian looked up at the prince, stunned. "I want to see your face when I take your medallion," Lumen boasted. He smiled and knocked the Insector's helmet off with his lance.

What the prince saw made his blood ran cold. This creature was *not* Centok. The Insector lacked the prominent brow ridges and blast antennae of Centipedian rulers. It was an imposter!

Lumen angrily yanked the bug commander's life force medallion from his carapace. The creature disappeared into a cloud of reddish mist. The prince remounted his spider, his mind swirling.

"If that wasn't Centok, where is he?" Lumen wondered.

"I don't know," Ebony's mind answered back. The prince felt the spider's rising panic, an echo of his own.

"How could the Insectors think of this type of plan?" Lumen asked his steed. "They've never done anything like this before!"

Before Ebony could form an answer, the prince sensed the truth. The sinister hand of Mantid the Malevolent lurked behind this strategy.

Centipedians swarmed in around the prince. They yipped and chittered joyfully, happy to have the Spider Rider leader cut off from the rest of his compatriots.

Ebony and Lumen tried to leap away, but the bugs grabbed the spider's legs, weighing him down.

"We'll have to fight our way back!" Ebony mind-talked to Lumen.

Lumen slashed around them with his lance, but his mind wasn't fully concentrating on the task. Worry built inside his gut. Where was Centok? Why was a decoy leading the Centipedian army?

Thunder shattered the air and lightning flashed.

Startled, the prince looked toward the city. Spider Riders scattered as bright white energy scorched through their ranks.

From the jungle at the back of the plateau emerged *another* Centipedian army. At its head came a huge weapon unlike anything Lumen had seen before.

It looked like a crystal rod with a huge metal sphere on the end. Metal rings encircled the weapon's glowing shaft. The device rested on a sturdy wheeled platform, moved forward by dozens of Centipedians. The front end of the weapon smoked slightly; the air stank of lightning.

"It's a lightning thrower!" Ebony echoed in Lumen's mind. This was what had made the noise and caused the other Spider Riders to scatter!

With the riders dazed and regrouping, only a small contingent of Turandot militia stood between the lightning thrower and the city. Behind the weapon rode a tall Centipedian. His armor and his scorpion mount both glistened red, like blood. The Insector laughed as he led his troops forward.

With a jolt of horror, Prince Lumen realized that his forces had been outflanked. While he and the others tried to drive the decoy army off, Centok—the *real* Centok—was attacking the city from the rear!

*

Igneous and his riders did not stop for rest as they rushed back to the city. They ate and drank on spiderback, never slowing from a full gallop.

Hunter Steele clung tight to Shadow's hair and tried to stay sitting upright. He wasn't really used to traveling this way yet, but he became more skilled with every passing mile.

The relentless pace took a toll on Hunter. Several times he fell asleep, only to be gently prodded awake by mind talk from Shadow. The never-changing position of the Inner World sun made it hard for him to gauge how long they'd traveled. It might have been a week, for all Hunter knew.

Just as Hunter thought he couldn't ride any more, they came within sight of the city. A huge Centipedian army was massed on the Arachnian plateau.

Igneous frowned. "They're fighting on two fronts," he said aloud.

"That's odd," Corona noted. "Centipedians usually attack in mass."

"I'm not liking this at all," Magma said. "Something isn't right here."

"It's Mantid," Petra concluded. "He's the one who's planned this attack."

"Shadow says he can't understand the city spiders yet," Hunter said. "Are any of the rest of you getting anything?"

"Just vague impressions," Corona replied.

"Flame's starting to pick things up," Igneous said. His face grew even grimmer. "Prince Lumen is caught in the middle of the Centipedian army."

"What's he doing there?" Magma asked. He seemed more annoyed than worried for the prince.

"He tried to capture Centok, but it was only a decoy," Igneous replied. The rider commander kept the others moving as fast as they could toward the city.

Petra nodded. "The bug leader always did like letting others do his dirty work."

Suddenly, thunder shook the air, and a huge flash of light lit up the sky.

"What was that?" Hunter asked.

"The Centipedians have a new weapon," Corona said. "It's some kind of lightning thrower."

"We'll split into three groups," Igneous commanded. "My group will go to help the prince. Petra, your group will find some way to stop that new weapon. Hunter and Princess Sparkle, while we distract the bugs, you'll sneak into the city and return the shard to the Oracle."

"But I can fight—" Hunter began.

"The Oracle is the most important now," Igneous said. "Without her help, the city may fall. The shard can restore a portion of her protection to Arachnia."

"Don't argue," Shadow cautioned Hunter. "There'll be plenty of time for heroics later."

"Hunter and I won't fail," Sparkle said, though doubt filled her young eyes.

As they grew closer to the plateau, all the spiders began to hear the telepathic voices of their compatriots. Hunter felt Shadow's anger rising as they swept forward. The spider wanted to charge into the Centipedians even more than Hunter did.

"Remember the plan," Hunter cautioned.

"Yesss," Shadow hissed. "I remember. Once the shard is safe, though..."

As the others charged forward, Hunter and Sparkle paused in the jungle. In an instant, their armor and their spiders' armor changed colors to camouflage them.

The princess trembled as she adjusted her stance on Hotarla.

"Don't worry, princess," Hunter said. He smiled, though he didn't feel much more confident than she did.

Sparkle checked the shard package that Igneous had given them, then said, "Let's go."

The princess and Hunter moved as quickly as they could through the jungle near the city's southwest edge. Ahead, they heard the clash of weapons and the shouts of warriors—both human and Centipedian.

The cries of the Turandot spiders echoed through their minds as well. The telepathy gave the riders an edge, but they were still badly outnumbered. Hunter hoped that Corona and the rest would be okay.

He and Sparkle reached the edge of the jungle. A wide contingent of Centipedians stood between them and the cliff face. To their left, Igneous and the others rode to help Prince Lumen. To their right, Petra and her legion galloped to cut off the lightning thrower.

"Ready?" Hunter asked.

Sparkle nodded nervously.

Z-ZAM!

The bug weapon fired again. A bolt of green-white light streaked over the armies and struck the city battlement atop the cliff. The walls of Arachnia began to crumble.

25
Lightning Attack

"We have to move quickly," Hunter said to Sparkle.

"I know," Sparkle snapped. "Hotarla already mentioned it. Use mind talk! You want someone to hear us?"

Hunter shook his head. He still wasn't used to being able to send telepathic messages to the other riders. Being mind-linked with a spider still gave him the creeps sometimes, too.

"Oh, that's very nice," Shadow commented sarcastically.

Hunter cursed himself for not hiding his thoughts more deeply. "Sorry," he thought, trying to mean it. "Have Hotarla tell Sparkle we'll go on my signal."

"Too late!" Shadow said.

The young princess and her spider lunged forward, heading for the base of the city's plateau. Hotarla was young and therefore very small by Turandot spider standards. Much of the time, she had to struggle to keep going under the princess's weight.

The ride to find Igneous had taken a lot out of the young duo, too, yet they lurched forward as fast as they could. A mask of grim determination fell over Sparkle's face.

"Will they make it?" Hunter wondered.

"Not if we don't help them," Shadow replied.

A gang of roving Centipedians spotted the princess and her spider. They hissed and charged in her direction, waving their clubs, spears, and rough-hewn swords.

"Tell Sparkle to keep going!" Hunter thought to Shadow. "We'll hold off the 'pedes."

"My pleasure," Shadow thought back.

As the 'pedes rushed in, Hunter and Shadow turned to meet them. Power from Hunter's manacle surged through his lance. He ignored the flashing power crystal. Hunter knew he'd have to make do with what little manacle energy remained. He resolved not to use his sonic charge unless absolutely necessary.

Shadow landed right in the middle of the advancing Centipedians. Their weapons bent and shattered against the Turandot spider's armor. Hunter clouted a half dozen with his lance. He'd trained with it a bit during the journey back to the city, but his basic technique was still to swing it like a giant baseball bat.

He and Shadow scattered the attacking bugs, then raced back to Sparkle's side. She and Hotarla reached the edge of the cliff and began climbing.

"Push yourself, Hotarla!" Hunter heard Shadow think.

"What's wrong?" Hunter asked.

"Hotarla is almost exhausted," Shadow replied. "She doubts she can make it."

"Maybe we can help," Hunter thought.

"How?"

"By giving her a tow."

"I see the plan in your mind," Shadow said. "It might work."

He raced ahead of the younger spider and shot a web line to her.

Hotarla grabbed the line, and Shadow dragged her up the cliff face toward the city wall. The big spider grunted with the effort, but he did not complain. As they reached the base of the cliff-top wall, Sparkle and Hotarla looked considerably less winded.

"Almost there!" Hunter said.

Suddenly, fire burst all around them. Sparkle shrieked and Shadow lost his footing on the lightning-cracked wall. The big spider and Hunter fell off the cliff face toward the centipede army below.

"What happened?" Hunter cried as they fell.

"Fire catapult," Shadow replied. "Hang on!"

He shot out a web line. The sticky rope latched onto the cliff face and jerked them to a stop. They swung back onto the rock. Shadow deftly cushioned their landing with his eight legs. Hunter grunted and tried not to fall off.

"Good job!" he said. "Are you all right?"

"Yes," the spider replied. "Venus tried to alert me, but her warning came just a moment too late. She and Corona are fighting on the plain nearby."

Hunter looked toward the top of the cliff. A sticky ball of fiery pitch clung to the sheer rock face above them. The smoke and flame blocked his view. "Are Sparkle and Hotarla okay?" he asked.

"They're scared but all right," Shadow replied. "They let go when the blast came. They're making their way to the top of the wall."

Hunter swung his gaze to the centipede ranks. He spotted the fire catapult taking aim once more. "Let's get them before they can shoot at the princess again."

Shadow raced down the wall and charged into the Insectors. He bulled through their ranks, shoving them aside as he went. Hunter used his lance to bat away any weapons that looked as though they might get through.

The 'pedes desperately swung the catapult toward Hunter and his spider.

"Duck!" Shadow thought. But Hunter was way ahead of him. As the catapult fired, both spider and rider flattened. The fiery ball of pitch sailed over their heads and burst amid the Centipedians behind them. The burning 'pedes screamed and fled to put out the fire.

Before the catapult crew could reload, Hunter pounced. Shadow bowled the Centipedians over. He caught the leader of the crew in his jaw and flung him through the air.

Hunter brought the blade of his lance down on the rope used to wind and load the catapult. The rope snapped, rendering the weapon useless. Hunter toppled a brazier of burning pitch onto the wooden structure, for good measure. Sticky flaming liquid spread over the catapult's wooden surface.

"They won't be getting near *that* any time soon," Hunter said with satisfaction. He glanced back toward the cliff. "Sparkle's almost over the wall!" he said.

"Not everyone is doing so well," Shadow warned. "Look."

A mental tug in Hunter's mind made him turn in the direction the spider wanted. Ahead of them, Petra and her squad battled to reach the lightning thrower. They'd made some progress, but the mass of Insectors facing them remained very thick.

The lightning cannon pivoted and blasted at Petra and her legion.

Petra and her spider leaped out of the way, but the rest of her crew went down, shocked insensate by the terrible weapon. Many of the surrounding Insectors fell, too. Centok laughed, not caring that he'd blasted so many of his own forces. He swung the weapon toward the crumbling cliff-top wall once more.

"We have to help Petra!" Hunter said.

"Yes," Shadow agreed. "Sparkle can handle the shard on her own."

They raced forward, through the line of fallen Insectors.

Petra leaped up, jabbing her lance at Centok. The enemy commander fended off her blow with his curve-bladed spear. His bodyguards swarmed in around the hurt and tired Spider Rider.

The rest of Centok's flanking army closed ranks, cutting Hunter and Shadow off. Hunter smashed them aside with his lance. Shadow scattered many with his eight legs and threw others into the air with his powerful jaws. But too many Insectors remained for Hunter to reach Petra quickly.

Centok's scorpion mount got in a lucky sting. Its tail lashed into one of the soft leg joints of Petra's mount. The spider squealed so loudly that Hunter heard her in his mind across the link he shared with Shadow.

Petra and her spider lurched back. They sprayed webbing at Centok to buy themselves some time. The Centipedian commander and his mount skittered out of the way. The webbing sailed past Centok and landed on the front end of the lightning thrower, just as it fired again.

Green-white energy coursed through the air, smashing into the wall of the city. The wall quaked and then crumbled, leaving a huge hole at its base—plenty of room for Centok's army to swarm inside.

But the blast had another effect as well.

When it fired, some of the cannon's energy arced through Petra's webbing, back to her and her spider. A second sound like thunder shook the air.

Petra and her spider stood rigidly for a moment, every hair on their bodies standing on end. Then they went limp and fell to the ground.

The Centipedian army swarmed over them.

26
Hunter Fights Alone

"No!" Hunter cried. He urged Shadow forward, and the big spider leaped as he had never leaped before.

Shadow rocketed over the intervening Insectors and landed at Petra's side. Hunter smashed with his lance as Shadow flailed with his legs and gnashed with his mandibles. They quickly drove the bug warriors back from the pale, unmoving bodies of Petra and her spider.

"Are they dead?" Hunter thought to Shadow.

"I don't know," Shadow replied. "I can't hear Petra's spider. She doesn't reply to me." For a moment, Hunter and Shadow's concern for their fallen comrades blotted out everything else.

They turned barely in time to parry the sting of Centok's red scorpion. The Insector chief had sneaked up on them while they were worrying. Now he and his mount surged forward, attacking with pincers, tail, and curved spear.

"Take them!" Centok commanded his troops. "They are all that stands between us and Arachnia!"

The other Centipedians swarmed forward again, slashing and stabbing, trying to bring rider and spider down.

Shadow lashed out with his eight legs. It was all he could do to keep the warrior bugs off them. The scorpion's sting arced toward Shadow's head. Hunter batted it aside with his lance and stabbed at Centok.

The scorpion caught Hunter's weapon with its claws. It twisted hard, nearly pulling Hunter off Shadow's back.

"Hunter, look out!"

Shadow's warning came almost too late. The Centipedian commander swung around with his spear, aiming for Hunter's head. Hunter ducked slightly at the last instant. Only the spear's shaft hit him, but the force was still enough to knock him silly.

The world swam around Hunter. He felt himself falling... falling just as he had through the lava tube that had taken him to the Inner World. For a moment, everything went black.

Then he felt as though bees were living in his head. The whole world seemed alive with buzzing and clatter and shouting.

"Hunter, wake up!"

Shadow's cry pierced the veil of darkness surrounding the boy. Hunter opened his eyes and found himself lying face-down on the battlefield.

Shadow stood over him, protecting him from the swarming Centipedians.

"Centok's climbing the wall!" Shadow shouted in his mind. "You have to get up!"

"What about the others?" Hunter gasped.

"They're too far away to help," Shadow replied. "We're the only ones who can reach Centok before he enters the city."

Hunter struggled to his feet. He had to lean heavily against the spider to remain standing. The whole world seemed to consist of pain and noise and swirling lights. His skull throbbed and his muscles ached. His eyes ran across the many scrapes and dings in his spider's armor. Shadow, too, was nearly exhausted. Hunter tried to bring up his lance, tried to focus on the battle, but it all seemed unreal to him.

Slowly, he crawled onto the spider's back.

The Insector army, with Centok in the lead, swarmed up the cliff.

"We're too late!" Hunter realized. "He's going to reach the city!"

Centok raised his spear in triumph as he led his troops toward the breach in the wall. The antennae atop his head crackled with malevolent power.

"Go, Shadow! Go!" Hunter thought. He felt the exhausted spider's pain as Shadow loped toward the base of the cliff.

"You're right," the arachnid thought sorrowfully. "We're not going to make it!"

"We have to try!"

As they began climbing the cliff, Centok reached the huge hole in the city wall.

But suddenly, a blue-white shimmer like summer lightning flashed through the sky above Arachnia. Centok stopped abruptly, as though he'd run into an invisible barrier.

Blue sparks flew up where the Insectors touched the city wall. The Centipedians shrieked in pain and surprise. The bug army reeled back. Some of them toppled off the cliff face to their doom.

Centok roared with anger. His antennae flashed with green light as he attacked the unseen barrier. The malevolent burst of energy stopped short of the city, like a wave breaking against the shore.

"Sparkle's done it!" Shadow cried in Hunter's mind. "She's restored the shard!"

Hunter's heart soared. "Let's get them!" he cried.

The earth-born Spider Rider surged forward, into the mass of confused Insectors. He and Shadow lashed out with all their strength. They knocked dozens of Centipedians from the cliff face, slowly working their way toward Centok.

Centok and his scorpion scrambled down the cliff, ignoring the advancing boy and spider. The 'pede commander's raspy voice boomed across the battlefield. "Bring the lightning thrower!" He pointed toward the opening in the city wall. "Their defenses will not long withstand its might!"

The Centipedians wheeled the lightning cannon to the base of the cliff and pointed it at the breach in the wall.

"Is he right?" Hunter asked Shadow. A Centipedian swung its sword at his head. Hunter ducked and knocked it off the cliff with his lance.

"I . . . I don't know," Shadow replied. "The Oracle is not at full power. The city shield may not be able to withstand this weapon."

"Then we have to stop it," Hunter said.

"How?" Shadow asked. He clouted two Centipedians in the head with his forelimbs as he raced back down the cliff face toward the lightning thrower.

"Jump on the cannon," Hunter said.

"What?" Shadow said. "You saw what it did to Petra!"

"Exactly," Hunter said. "Trust me. I know it will work."

Having overcome their surprise, the Centipedian army swarmed up the cliff at the boy and the spider once more.

Shadow sprang off the cliff face, aiming for the lightning cannon below. He arced through the air and landed lightly on the barrel of the device. His bulk almost covered the weapon's wide nozzle.

"If they fire this now," Shadow thought, "there'll be nothing left of us."

"Follow the plan!" Hunter urged.

Near the bottom of the cliff, Centok and his scorpion turned to face them. The Spider Rider's leap had surprised the Insector commander. He spurred his mount through his troops and galloped toward Hunter and Shadow. Centok's antennae glowed angrily, building power for a deadly blast.

The weapon glowed, too, as it built up lightning within its barrel. The device's energy made Hunter's skin tingle and his hair stand on end. He knew that Shadow felt it, too. It was like a million tiny bugs crawling all over them.

"Fire!" cried Centok. "Kill them!"

"Now!" Hunter shouted. "Spin your web and jump now!"

Shadow attached his web to the front of the lightning thrower. He leaped toward Centok, spinning a web line as he went.

Centok shot green energy at them as they came. Hunter barely deflected the burst with his shield. His arm went numb. "Come on!" he thought. "Come on! Shoot now!"

Shadow draped the end of his web over Centok as they flew past.

The lightning cannon fired.

The weapon's lightning coursed through the spiderweb, just as it had when it downed Petra. The webbing covering the cannon's nose sent the energy back into the weapon. The cannon exploded from the feedback.

Simultaneously, the rest of the charge raced down the line Shadow had cast over the centipede leader.

Centok shrieked in agony as electricity coursed through the web into his armored body. His scorpion flailed wildly as the cannon's power electrified it, as well. The villain and his mount lit up like neon signs. Their exoskeletons glowed black and orange. They shook uncontrollably for a few moments, then fell, smoking, to the ground.

Hunter almost shouted with glee. But Shadow had not gotten far enough away from the charged web line. As the cannon's lightning electrocuted the Centipedian leader, it also arced from the web into him and Hunter.

Pain like fire shot through every fiber of Hunter's body. Thunder roared in his ears. White light burst behind his eyes.

Then everything went black.

27
A Hero's Welcome

"Hunter, come back!" someone said.

It was a pleasant voice, one Hunter recognized.

"Shadow?" he asked.

"No," the voice replied. "It's me."

The darkness drew back as the world swam into focus once more.

"It's me," the girl standing over him repeated, "Corona." She was scraped and bruised but otherwise okay. She was wearing her pedestrian clothing, not her armor.

Hunter tried to smile but found that every muscle in his body ached. "I thought I was dead," he moaned.

"You very nearly were," she replied. "Fortunately, I heard you cry out after the lightning machine hit you. I had enough power in my manacle to use the healing hand function. Without it, I doubt you would have pulled through."

Hunter sat up abruptly, which made his head throb with pain. "What about Shadow?" he asked.

"I'm here," said the spider's voice in his mind. "I'm recovering. Spiders are tougher to kill than humans, and the city has some excellent arachnid physicians. Now, if you don't mind, I'd like to get some rest."

"Where are the others?" Hunter asked Corona.

"When Centok fell, the Centipedians panicked," she said. "Many fled back to their homeland. Prince Lumen, Igneous,

Magma, and the rest are tracking down and dispatching those that remain."

"So everyone else came through okay," Hunter said, managing a smile.

Corona nodded. "Well, there are a few other riders here in the infirmary, and...." She took a deep breath.

"And...?" Hunter said. Then he realized. "Petra! Are she and the rest of the legion okay?"

"The rest, yes," Corona said. "But Petra..."

Despite his aches and pains, Hunter forced himself out of bed. "Take me to her," he said.

Corona supported his arm and took him into an adjoining chamber. Physicians bustled quietly around the room, looking very serious. Petra lay on her back on a bed in the chamber's center. Her eyes stared at the ceiling. Her skin was very pale. Hunter had to look hard to see that she was breathing.

The king stood at her bedside, holding her hand. Princess Sparkle, still wearing her smudged and dirty clothes, stood beside him, weeping.

"Her life is slipping away," the king said. "If the Oracle were whole, we would have the power to heal her, but...." He shook his head sadly.

"There must be something you can do!" Hunter said. A hard lump formed in his throat, and he had to fight to keep from crying.

"There is one thing," King Arachna said. "It is a last resort, and we have never tried it before. Those enemies who cannot be dispatched by taking their life force medallions, we put in sleep webs. These webs suspend the life of the prisoner. Those inside need neither food nor water. They sleep endlessly. Even aging is slowed."

He looked at the gravely wounded rider. "Cocooning Petra is the only way to save her life. We will send her to the Hall of Heroes and keep her safe against the day when—the Oracle willing—we may revive her." He took a deep breath and sighed it out. "She may have to sleep a long time."

"At least until the other shards of the Oracle are recovered," Corona added.

Hunter nodded and sighed. The life of a Spider Rider could be good, but it was also very dangerous. He reminded himself never to forget that. If he did, he would lose any chance of returning to the surface world.

Corona took his hand and led him out of the chamber.

"We'll get those shards," Hunter told her. "We'll revive Petra one day."

Corona looked into his confident eyes and nodded. "I'm sure we will," Corona said. "For now, you should return to the infirmary."

Wearily, Hunter agreed.

They walked through the palace back to the medical wing. There they found a small contingent of riders waiting for them. Magma, Igneous, and Prince Lumen smiled as Hunter and Corona entered the room.

The two older riders looked little the worse for wear. Prince Lumen, though, sported a fresh cut on his forehead above his left eye. As a physician bandaged his wound, the prince smiled at Hunter.

"So, the hero returns!" Magma said heartily. "We were a bit worried when we didn't find you here, in bed."

"Hero?" Hunter said, puzzled.

"It was your defeat of Centok and his lightning thrower

that saved the day," Igneous said. "A clever strategy. How did you think of it, by the way?"

"When Petra got zapped, I realized what to do," Hunter said, "I'd seen something like what I did about a million times on TV."

"TV?" the prince asked.

"It's an entertainment we have in the surface world," Hunter explained. "Sort of like a having a theater in a tiny box."

"It sounds wondrous," Corona said.

"Sometimes," Hunter agreed. "Except for the commercials."

Everyone in the room looked puzzled. Hunter laughed.

"Well," Lumen said, "wherever the idea came from, well done." He stepped forward and patted Hunter on the shoulder. Looking at Igneous, he added, "I don't think anyone will question my decision to make you a Spider Rider now."

"No one would ever question your leadership, my prince," Igneous said graciously. He bowed.

Lumen nodded his head to Igneous and smiled. "Nor yours, captain-general."

"Before these two flatter each other to death," Magma said, "we have something for you." He extended his right hand to Hunter. In it, he held a round object.

"It's Centok's life force medallion," Lumen explained. "A fitting start to your trophy collection."

"You were busy being injured at the time," Magma said, "so we had to collect it for you. I hope you don't mind."

"Not at all," Hunter said, taking the life force medallion from him.

"Now, by royal decree, I order you to rest and recover," Prince Lumen said. "We may have won the day, but the war with the Insectors is not yet over. There are still shards to recover, still battles to be fought."

Hunter saluted him. "I'll be happy to fight them beside you," he said, "all of you." He gazed around the room at his new friends. He'd known these people only a few weeks, but right now, he couldn't imagine living without them. Hunter Steele smiled.

"I may never get home," he thought to himself, "but at least I've found a place here, in Arachnia. Even the spiders aren't so bad—once you get used to them."

"Well, thanks a lot," Shadow said in his mind.

"Hey!" Hunter thought back. "I thought you were sleeping."

"Turandot spiders never really rest," Shadow said. "And neither do Spider Riders."

Hunter Steele laughed, looking forward to the many adventures to come.

Tedd Anasti and Patsy Cameron-Anasti

Tedd and Patsy met when Tedd was producing live-action children's shows for Walt Disney Studios and Patsy auditioned for a role in one of his episodes. They discovered a mutual love for quality children's entertainment and became writing partners. Their first show as a team was the Emmy Award–winning series *The Smurfs* for Hanna-Barbera.

Over the next two decades, Tedd and Patsy wrote and produced more than 500 half hours of such children's television hits as Disney's *Timon and Pumbaa, Duck Tales*, and *The Little Mermaid*. They also wrote and produced the *Free Willy* television series for Warner Brothers and received their second Emmy Award for Tim Burton's *Beetlejuice*. Tedd and Patsy have received eight Emmy nominations, three Humanitas Prize nominations, the Governor's Media Award, and the Silver Angel Award for Excellence in Children's Television.

Tedd and Patsy have two children, Emily Rose and Teddy. It was their son's passion for spiders that inspired *Spider Riders*.

One day, Teddy, then only five, announced that he had captured ten black widows in their backyard in California. At first, Tedd and Patsy didn't believe their son had really captured black widows, but upon inspection found that it was true!

In order to get the boy to turn his deadly black widows in to the local nature center, Tedd and Patsy agreed to buy Teddy two nonpoisonous tarantulas—one male, one female. The Anasti household is now a tarantula breeding ground!

The Spider Boy, as he is known, became a hero to the other kids in the neighborhood. Upon seeing how fascinated children are with spiders, Tedd and Patsy were inspired to write the novel *Spider Riders*—the story of a boy lost in a primitive underground world of warring giant insects where his best friend is a ten-foot battle spider.